玩遊戲學單字！

英文中級單字
藏在格子裡
【輕鬆戰勝英檢中級】

```
        C
    M   A
    E M P T Y     S
    S   A         I
    S   B     M   O   D Y
            
A D M I R E               T
```

U0074066

使用說明 User's Guide

邊玩邊學英文單字！英檢中級輕鬆考！

全民英檢好難考？英文單字量永遠不夠？背越多、忘越多嗎？
現在就要讓你從遊戲中，**輕鬆學單字**！全民英檢**一次過關**！

英文單字量不夠、單字背過就忘、背單字好枯燥……都是許多英語學習者共同的困擾，也是面對考試時最頭痛的問題。本書精選了**1520個**英檢中級必考的單字，組合成**95題填字遊戲**，讓你從玩遊戲中累積中級英檢的通關本事！

國外流行多年！現在讓你
邊玩邊學單字填字遊戲，輕鬆考英檢！

填字遊戲有兩種方向的提示，**ACROSS**是指橫向單字，**DOWN**是指直向單字，每個**橫向**跟**直向**單字前面都有數字編號，只要**參考提示**，並依據提示的編號，對應到格子裡的編號，再**填入答案**就行了！每個單字都會和另一個單字**共用**某個字母，因此，即使一時間想不到某個單字，也可以透過其他已填好的單字去**聯想**，單字量自然累積！

◎ 捷徑文化版權所有

◆用KK音標猜猜英文單字

橫向提示

ACROSS

3 [ˈmægnɪt]
4 [ˈhɔrbɚ]
5 [ˈrezɚ]
6 [ˈlædɚ]
8 [ˌɪlɛkˈtrɪsətɪ]
10 [ˈdʒuəlrɪ]
13 [ˈtruθfəl]
14 [ˈtjutɚ]
15 [pɚˈswed]

依照提示填入答案

直向單字

DOWN

1 [siz]
2 [ˈlɔndrɪ]
3 [ˈmænɪdʒmənt]
7 [parˈtɪsəˌpet]
9 [ˈfitʃɚ]
11 [ˈkɛtl]
12 [ˈvɑljəm]

◆上面的遊戲會用到的單字都在這裡！真的看不懂提示就來偷瞄一下吧！

WORD BANK: Electricity, feature, harbor, jewelry, kettle, ladder, laundry, magnet, management, participate,

Word Bank 提供當回所有單字，
要你增強信心，一個字都不放過！

如果真的猜不透遊戲提示，下方的**Word Bank**也列出當回遊戲中的所有單字，**多一層線索、少一分難度**，讓挫折感消失，信心滿滿，越玩越得意！

四大分類切入單字學習，
怎麼玩也不膩！怎麼考都難不倒你！

全書填字遊戲，分成**四部分**，分別以**KK音標、中文翻譯、英文例句、英英解釋**四種不同方式作提示，可依自己能力及對單字理解度**循序漸進**地玩，在遊戲中自然而然**全方位理解**單字的意義及用法；**不同的遊戲規則**也讓你不會輕易厭倦，學習樂趣最高！

每回遊戲後，立即揭曉答案，
馬上學習，印象加倍，功力雙倍！

每回遊戲後，下一頁立即揭曉答案，再也沒有翻來翻去的麻煩！馬上複習所有單字，印象更加深刻！不僅告訴你中文意思，更有音標教你發音，以及英英解釋幫助你精準地掌握此字的意義，強化記憶，就是要你牢牢記住它！單字功力瞬間飆破表！

◆單字還記不熟嗎？快來做複習！

fable [ˈfebl] 寓言 a short story that teaches a lesson or reality	**racial** [ˈreʃəl] 種族的 of or connected with a person's race
grocery [ˈgrosərɪ] 雜貨店 a shop of a grocer	**regional** [ˈridʒənl] 區域性的 of or in a particular region

附贈全書填字遊戲線上下載，
讓你隨時隨地，想玩就玩！

怕玩過一次就不能再玩了嗎？擔心寫在書上會弄得又髒又亂嗎？想要和朋友現場PK誰最先填完所有格子嗎？本書貼心**附贈全書填字遊戲完整PDF檔**（見封面QR code），讓你想玩就列印出來，隨時隨地都能帶著走、到處玩！反覆練習，學習效果永不間斷，單字再也不會背了就忘！

前言 Preface

　　全民英檢（GEPT）是台灣英語學習者最重要的英語檢定測驗之一，除了分成初級、中級、中高級、高級四種難度，還囊括了聽、說、讀、寫四種語言能力的檢測：第一階段「初試」測驗聽力、閱讀，第二階段「複試」測驗口說、寫作。這對許多英語學習者來說，有其相當的難度！尤其不論是測試哪一項能力，單字絕對是最基礎的一環，也是奪得高分的關鍵！常聽到學習者抱怨：會的單字太少，聽力無法完全理解！閱讀總是遇到不會的單字就卡住、文章怎麼讀都不懂！口說、寫作都因為太多單字不會，而無法流利地表達怎麼辦？

　　背單字這件事，對許多英語學習者來說都很頭痛，英文單字到底有多少個？英文單字量到底要多少才夠？單字要怎麼樣才不會背了就忘？其實單字學習只要用對方法，就能事倍功半！秉持著「教大家用充滿樂趣的方式學英文、在遊戲中學習」的理念，設計了這本續作《英文中級單字藏在格子裡》，就是要讓大家在遊戲中背單字、增加字彙量，輕鬆征服英檢中級考試！

　　這本《英文中級單字藏在格子裡》絕對要破除你對背單字的恐懼，讓你從遊戲中自然記憶單字，以KK音標、中文意思、英英解釋、英文例句四種不同的提示方式做分類，讓你全面掌握單字學習！每回遊戲完，解答頁立刻幫你做完整複習，音標、中文意思、英英解釋一併呈現，快速加深印象！隨書附贈的光碟，更能讓你反覆練習、和同學朋友一起競賽、刺激學習動機，從此背英文單字再也難不倒你，全民英檢輕鬆過關！

目錄 Contents

Level 1

用KK音標提示玩單字

1

◉ 捷徑文化版權所有

◆用KK音標猜猜英文單字

ACROSS

- 3 [ˋmægnɪt]
- 4 [ˋhɑrbɚ]
- 5 [ˋrezɚ]
- 6 [ˋlædɚ]
- 8 [ɪˏlɛkˋtrɪsətɪ]
- 10 [ˋdʒuəlrɪ]
- 13 [ˋtruθfəl]
- 14 [ˋtjutɚ]
- 15 [pɚˋswed]

DOWN

- 1 [siz]
- 2 [ˋlɔndrɪ]
- 3 [ˋmænɪdʒmənt]
- 7 [pɑrˋtɪsəˏpet]
- 9 [ˋfitʃɚ]
- 11 [ˋkɛtl̩]
- 12 [ˋvaljəm]

◆上面的遊戲會用到的單字都在這裡！真的看不懂提示就來偷瞄一下吧！

WORD BANK: Electricity, feature, harbor, jewelry, kettle, ladder, laundry, magnet, management, participate, persuade, razor, seize, truthful, tutor, volume.

答案就在後面

◆填字遊戲解答在這裡！

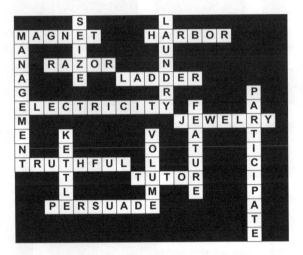

◆單字還記不熟嗎？快來做複習！

electricity [ɪˌlɛkˈtrɪsətɪ] 電 the power which is produced by various means and which provides heat and light, drives machines	**management** [ˈmænɪdʒmənt] 處理、管理 the art or practice of managing
feature [ˈfitʃɚ] 特徵、特色 a typical part or quality	**participate** [pɑrˈtɪsəˌpet] 參加 to take part
harbor [ˈhɑrbɚ] 港口 an area of water by a coast which is sheltered from rougher waters so that ships are safe inside it	**persuade** [pɚˈswed] 說服 to make someone willing to do something
jewelry [ˈdʒuəlrɪ] 珠寶 body decorations such as rings and necklaces	**razor** [ˈrezɚ] 刮鬍刀、剃刀 a sharp instrument for removing hair
kettle [ˈkɛtḷ] 水壺 a metal or plastic container with a lid, a handle, and a spout, used mainly for heating water	**seize** [siz] 抓、抓住 to grab tightly
ladder [ˈlædɚ] 梯子 a structure consisting of two bars or ropes joined to each other by steps and used for climbing	**truthful** [ˈtruθfəl] 誠實的 being very honest
laundry [ˈlɔndrɪ] 洗衣店、送洗的衣服 a place or business where clothes are washed and ironed	**tutor** [ˈtjutɚ] 家庭教師、導師 a teacher who gives private instruction to a single pupil
magnet [ˈmægnɪt] 磁鐵 a piece of iron which can make other metal objects come towards	**volume** [ˈvɑljəm] 卷、冊、音量、容積 loudness of sound, the degree, strength

2

◉ 捷徑文化版權所有

◆用KK音標猜猜英文單字

ACROSS

- 3 [ˈgrosərɪ]
- 5 [ˈhɛvən]
- 12 [ˌapəˈtjunətɪ]
- 13 [ˌpaləˈtɪʃən]
- 14 [wɔrmθ]
- 15 [ˈreʃəl]
- 16 [ˈfebl̩]

DOWN

- 1 [ˈskɛrˌkro]
- 2 [sɪˈkjurətɪ]
- 4 [jɔn]
- 6 [smuð]
- 7 [ˌɪndəˈvɪdʒuəl]
- 8 [ˈstɛpˌtʃɪld]
- 9 [ˈrɪdʒənl̩]
- 10 [ˈminˌhwaɪl]
- 11 [ˈhɑrmfəl]

◆上面的遊戲會用到的單字都在這裡！真的看不懂提示就來偷瞄一下吧！

WORD BANK: Fable, grocery, harmful, heaven, individual, meanwhile, opportunity, politician, racial, regional, scarecrow, security, smooth, stepchild, warmth, yawn.

答案就在後面

Level-1

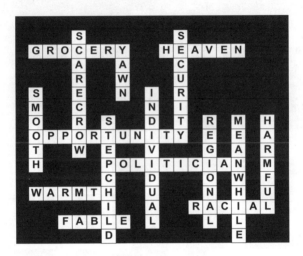

◆單字還記不熟嗎？快來做複習！

fable [ˈfebl̩] 寓言 a short story that teaches a lesson	**racial** [ˈreʃəl] 種族的 of or connected with a person's race
grocery [ˈgrosərɪ] 雜貨店 a shop of a grocer	**regional** [ˈridʒənl̩] 區域性的 of or in a particular region
harmful [ˈhɑrmfəl] 引起傷害的、有害的 causing or likely to cause harm	**scarecrow** [ˈskɛrˌkro] 稻草人 an object in the shape of a person, set up in a field to keep birds away from crops
heaven [ˈhɛvən] 天堂 the place where God is believed to live	**security** [sɪˈkjʊrətɪ] 安全 the state of being secured
individual [ˌɪndəˈvɪdʒʊəl] 個別的、個人 separate or particular	**smooth** [smuð] 平滑的 not rough
meanwhile [ˈminˌhwaɪl] 同時、期間 in the same time	**stepchild** [ˈstɛpˌtʃɪld] 前夫（妻）所生的孩子 a stepson or stepdaughter
opportunity [ˌɑpəˈtjunətɪ] 機會 a favorable moment	**warmth** [wɔrmθ] 暖和、溫暖、熱忱 the state or quality of being warm
politician [ˌpɑləˈtɪʃən] 政治家 a person whose business is politics	**yawn** [jɔn] 打呵欠、呵欠 to open the mouth widely and breathe deeply, as when tired or uninterested

3

◉ 捷徑文化版權所有

◆用KK音標猜猜英文單字

ACROSS

2 [ˋvaɪtəmɪn]
6 [ˋdʒɛləs]
10 [hʌʃ]
11 [ˋgʌvənə]
12 [ˋwægən]
13 [drʌŋk]
14 [ˋvaɪələns]

DOWN

1 [ˋgrin͵haʊs]
3 [ˋɪndʒərɪ]
4 [ɪnˋspɛktə]
5 [ˋglobl̩]
7 [ˋfæʃənəbl̩]
8 [ˋvɪvɪd]
9 [ˋnɪk͵nem]
10 [ˋhænd͵fʊl]
11 [ˋgælən]

◆上面的遊戲會用到的單字都在這裡！真的看不懂提示就來偷瞄一下吧！

WORD BANK: Drunk, fashionable, gallon, global, governor, greenhouse, handful, hush, injury, inspector, jealous, nickname, violence, vitamin, vivid, wagon.

答案就在後面

◆填字遊戲解答在這裡！

◆單字還記不熟嗎？快來做複習！

drunk [drʌŋk] 酒醉的、著迷的、醉漢 under the influence of alcohol	**injury** [ˈɪndʒərɪ] 傷害、損害 physical harm
fashionable [ˈfæʃənəbl̩] 流行的、時髦的 (made, dressed) according to the latest fashion	**inspector** [ɪnˈspɛktɚ] 視察員、檢查者 an official who is in charge of inspection
gallon [ˈgælən] 加侖 a measure for liquids	**jealous** [ˈdʒɛləs] 嫉妒的 unhappy and angry because you think that someone who should like you, like someone else better
global [ˈglobl̩] 球狀的、全球性的 ball-shaped; of or concerning the whole world	**nickname** [ˈnɪkˌnem] 綽號、暱稱 a name used informally instead of a person's own name
governor [ˈgʌvɚnɚ] 統治者 a person who controls any of certain types of organization or place	**violence** [ˈvaɪələns] 暴力 extreme force in action or feeling that causes damage, unrest
greenhouse [ˈgrinˌhaʊs] 溫室 a building with a glass roof and glass sides and often some form of heating, used for growing plants which need heat and light	**vitamin** [ˈvaɪtəmɪn] 維他命 any of several chemical substances which are found in very small quantities in certain foods, and are important for growth and good health
handful [ˈhændˌfʊl] 一把、少量 a small number	**vivid** [ˈvɪvɪd] 閃亮的、生動的 bright and strong; active in forming a lifelike image
hush [hʌʃ] 使寂靜、寂靜 to be silent and calm	**wagon** [ˈwægən] 四輪馬車、貨車 a strong four-wheeled road vehicle, mainly for heavy loads, drawn esp. by horses

4

◉ 捷徑文化版權所有

◆用KK音標猜猜英文單字

ACROSS

1 [ˈhɑrəbl̩]
4 [səˈfɪʃənt]
5 [ˈhɛdˌkwɔrtɚz]
9 [maɪˈnɔrətɪ]
10 [ˈdʒʌstɪs]
14 [kənˌsɪdəˈreʃən]
15 [ˈhwɪsl̩]
16 [ˈlɑbɪ]

DOWN

2 [ˈlaɪfˌtaɪm]
3 [friz]
6 [ˌmæθəˈmætɪkl̩]
7 [ʃæmˈpu]
8 [ˈtrænsport]
11 [skwiz]
12 [zon]
13 [ˈgæmbl̩]

◆上面的遊戲會用到的單字都在這裡！真的看不懂提示就來偷瞄一下吧！

WORD BANK: Consideration, freeze, gamble, headquarters, horrible, justice, lifetime, lobby, mathematical, minority, shampoo, squeeze, sufficient, transport, whistle, zone.

013

答案就在後面

◆填字遊戲解答在這裡！

◆單字還記不熟嗎？快來做複習！

consideration [kənˌsɪdəˈreʃən] 考慮 thoughtful attention to or care for the wishes, needs, or feelings of others	mathematical [ˌmæθəˈmætɪk!] 數學的 of or using mathematics
freeze [friz] 凍結 to harden as a result of extreme cold	minority [maɪˈnɔrətɪ] 少數 the smaller number
gamble [ˈgæmb!] 賭博 to risk on the result of something uncertain, such as a card game, a horse race, a business arrangement, etc	shampoo [ʃæmˈpu] 洗髮精 a liquid soap like product used for washing the hair
headquarters [ˈhɛdˌkwɔrtɚz] 總部、大本營 the central office where the people who work in can control a large organization	squeeze [skwiz] 壓搾、擠壓 to press firmly together
horrible [ˈhɔrəb!] 可怕的 very unpleasant	sufficient [səˈfɪʃənt] 足夠的 enough
justice [ˈdʒʌstɪs] 公平、公正 fairness	transport [ˈtrænsport] 運輸 a way to move things from one place to another
lifetime [ˈlaɪfˌtaɪm] 一生 the time during which a person is alive or a machine, organization, continues to exist	whistle [ˈhwɪs!] 哨子、口哨 a simple instrument for making a high sound by forcing air or steam through it
lobby [ˈlɑbɪ] 休息室、大廳 a wide hall or passage which leads from the entrance to the rooms inside a public building	zone [zon] 地區、地帶、劃分地區 a division or area marked off from others by particular qualities or activities

5

◉ 捷徑文化版權所有

◆用KK音標猜猜英文單字

ACROSS

3 [ˈhɛdˌlaɪn]
4 [ˈvɛrɪəs]
6 [ˈflevɚ]
10 [ˈsuəˌsaɪd]
12 [spɪˈsɪfɪk]
13 [ˈbiɪŋ]
14 [rɪˈsit]
15 [ˈnænɪ]

DOWN

1 [ˈθɪərɪ]
2 [ˈpevmənt]
3 [ˈhɛzəˌtet]
5 [rɪˈlaɪəbl]
7 [ˈlɪpˌstɪk]
8 [ˈgɑsəp]
9 [ˈlaɪfˌbot]
11 [ˈhændɪ]

◆上面的遊戲會用到的單字都在這裡！真的看不懂提示就來偷瞄一下吧！

WORD BANK: Being, flavor, gossip, handy, headline, hesitate, lifeboat, lipstick, nanny, pavement, receipt, reliable, specific, suicide, theory, various.

答案就在後面

◆填字遊戲解答在這裡！

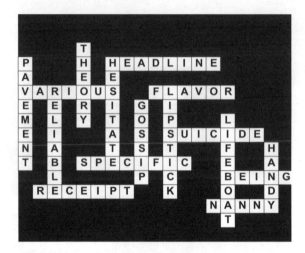

◆單字還記不熟嗎？快來做複習！

being [ˋbiɪŋ] 生命、存在 the state of existing	**nanny** [ˋnænɪ] 奶媽、保姆 a woman employed to take care of children in a family
flavor [ˋflevɚ] 味道、風味 a taste	**pavement** [ˋpevmənt] 人行道 a paved surface for pedestrians to walk on
gossip [ˋgɑsəp] 八卦、說閒話 conversations about the details of other people's behavior and private lives	**receipt** [rɪˋsit] 收據 a written statement that one has received money
handy [ˋhændɪ] 方便的、隨手可得的 useful and simple to use	**reliable** [rɪˋlaɪəbl̩] 可靠的 dependable
headline [ˋhɛdͺlaɪn] 標題 the heading printed in large letters above a story in a newspaper	**specific** [spɪˋsɪfɪk] 具體的、特殊的、明確的 detailed and exact
hesitate [ˋhɛzəͺtet] 遲疑、躊躇 to pause before taking an action or making decision	**suicide** [ˋsuəͺsaɪd] 自殺 the act of killing oneself
lifeboat [ˋlaɪfͺbot] 救生艇 a strong boat used for saving people in danger at sea	**theory** [ˋθiərɪ] 理論 a reasonable or scientifically acceptable explanation for a fact or event
lipstick [ˋlɪpͺstɪk] 口紅、唇膏 a cosmetic for brightening the color of the lips	**various** [ˋvɛrɪəs] 多種的 different from each other

6

◉ 捷徑文化版權所有

◆用KK音標猜猜英文單字

ACROSS

2 [ɪnˋstrʌkʃən]
4 [ˋonɚʃɪp]
6 [ˋdʒɛstʃɚ]
7 [klɪk]
9 [ˋwɪlo]
11 [ˋgrædʒuˏet]
14 [əˋkaʊnt]
16 [ˋsɔsɪdʒ]

DOWN

1 [ˋfɔrtʃən]
3 [gæŋ]
5 [ˋprivɪəs]
8 [naɪt]
10 [ˋaɪvərɪ]
12 [ˋtɪmbɚ]
13 [dʒel]
15 [gæp]

◆上面的遊戲會用到的單字都在這裡！真的看不懂提示就來偷瞄一下吧！

WORD BANK: Account, click, fortune, gang, gap, gesture, graduate, instruction, ivory, jail, knight, ownership, previous, sausage, timber, willow.

答案就在後面

◆填字遊戲解答在這裡！

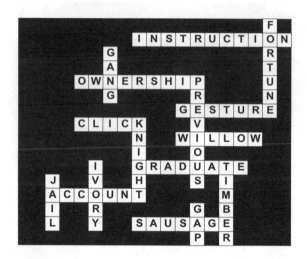

◆單字還記不熟嗎？快來做複習！

account [ə`kaʊnt] 帳目、描述 a sum of money kept in a bank	**ivory** [`aɪvərɪ] 象牙 a hard white substance of which an elephant's tusks are made
click [klɪk] 滴答聲、喀嚓聲 a slight short sound	**jail** [dʒel] 監獄 a place where prisons are kept
fortune [`fɔrtʃən] 運氣、財富 fate; a great amount of money	**knight** [naɪt] 騎士 a man of noble rank trained to fight, esp. on horseback
gap [gæp] 缺口、空隙 an empty space between two objects	**ownership** [`onɚʃɪp] 主權、所有權 sole right of possession
gang [gæŋ] 一隊（工人）、一群（囚犯） a group of	**previous** [`privɪəs] 先前的 happening or existing before the one mentioned
gesture [`dʒɛstʃɚ] 姿勢、手勢 a pose to show some expressions; to make gesture	**sausage** [`sɔsɪdʒ] 臘腸、香腸 a mixture of fresh or preserved meat with spices, and sometimes bread-like materials, in a tube of thin animal skin
graduate [`grædʒuˌet] 畢業生、畢業 a person who has completed a university degree course	**timber** [`tɪmbɚ] 木材、樹林 wood for building
instruction [ɪn`strʌkʃən] 指令、教導 an order; a direction	**willow** [`wɪlo] 柳樹 a type of tree which grows near water, with long thin branches

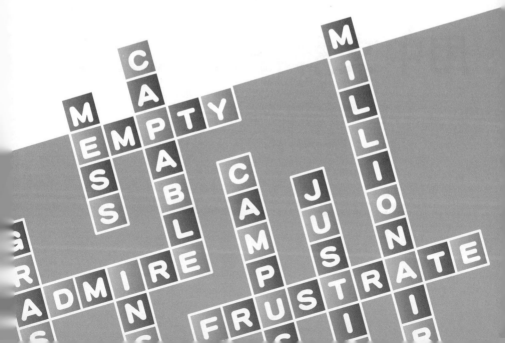

Level 2

用中文解釋提示玩單字

1

◉ 捷徑文化版權所有

◆用中文解釋猜猜英文單字

ACROSS

1 介系詞
4 完美
7 文學
11 依賴的
12 刺激、激發
13 困難的
15 平板、陪審團
16 蛋白質

DOWN

2 服從、遵從
3 值得尊敬的
5 演講
6 檢查、調查
8 獲得勝利
9 原始的、早期的
10 酬賞
14 口述的、口部的

◆上面的遊戲會用到的單字都在這裡！真的看不懂提示就來偷瞄一下吧！

WORD BANK: Dependent, inspection, lecture, literature, motivate, obedience, oral, panel, perfection, preposition, primitive, protein, respectable, reward, tough, triumph.

答案就在後面

◆填字遊戲解答在這裡！

```
P R E P O S I T I O N
    B                       R
  P E R F E C T I O N       E       L
    D                       S       E
    I     L I T E R A T U R E   P   C
  I N     E           R       P E   T
  N S     N           I     P R C   U
  S P   R C           U     R M T   R
D E P E N D E N T     M O T I V A T E
  C T   W             P     M B
  T I   A       T O U G H   I L
  I O   R       R           T E
  O N   D     P A N E L     I
  N           L             V
                P R O T E I N
```

◆單字還記不熟嗎？快來做複習！

dependent [dɪˋpɛndənt] 依賴的 relying on someone for the help	**perfection** [pɚˋfɛkʃən] 完美 the state of being perfect
inspection [ɪnˋspɛkʃən] 檢查、調查 to examine or look into something	**preposition** [ˏprɛpəˋzɪʃən] 介系詞 a word used with a noun, pronoun, or -ing form to show its connection with another word
lecture [ˋlɛktʃɚ] 演講 an informative talk given to a group of people	**primitive** [ˋprɪmətɪv] 原始的、早期的 of the earliest stage of development
literature [ˋlɪtərətʃɚ] 文學 written works that are regarded as having artistic value	**protein** [ˋprotiɪn] 蛋白質 one of the many natural substances found in food like meat, fish or eggs that is necessary for the body to grow and remain healthy
motivate [ˋmotəˏvet] 刺激、激發 make people willing to do work hard	**respectable** [rɪˋspɛktəbḷ] 值得尊敬的 showing standards of behavior or appearance that are socially acceptable
obedience [əˋbidjəns] 服從、遵從 when people do what they are told to do	**reward** [rɪˋwɔrd] 酬賞 a return for doing something good or valuable
oral [ˋorəl] 口述的、口部的 spoken, not written	**tough** [tʌf] 困難的 very difficult to deal with
panel [ˋpænḷ] 平板、陪審團 a separate division of the surface of a door, wall, or other structure, which is different in some way to the surface round it	**triumph** [ˋtraɪəmf] 獲得勝利 to gain a victory or success after a difficult struggle

2

◉ 捷徑文化版權所有

◆用中文解釋猜猜英文單字

ACROSS

3 接受
5 名詞
9 面部的、表面的
10 中斷、妨礙
13 目擊者、目擊
14 使硬化
15 技術上的
16 說明、解讀、翻譯

DOWN

1 支配、統治
2 紀念碑
4 徹底的
6 限制
7 強烈的、密集的
8 突出的
11 使恐懼、使驚嚇
12 打擊、一撞、撫摸

◆上面的遊戲會用到的單字都在這裡！真的看不懂提示就來偷瞄一下吧！

WORD BANK: Dominate, facial, harden, intensive, interpret, interruption, limitation, monument, noun, prominent, reception, stroke, technological, terrify, thorough, witness.

答案就在後面

◆填字遊戲解答在這裡！

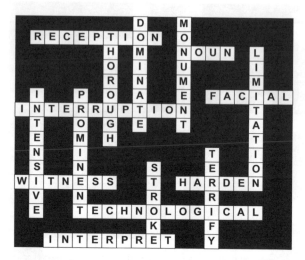

◆單字還記不熟嗎？快來做複習！

dominate [ˈdɑməˌnet] 支配、統治 to rule or control by superior power	**noun** [naʊn] 名詞 a word that can serve as the subject
facial [ˈfeʃəl] 面部的、表面的 on the face; relating to face	**prominent** [ˈprɑmənənt] 突出的 sticking or stretching out beyond a surface
harden [ˈhɑrdn̩] 使硬化 to make or become hard or stiff	**reception** [rɪˈsɛpʃən] 接受 a particular kind of welcome
intensive [ɪnˈtɛnsɪv] 強烈的、密集的 putting lots of attention or effort in a short period of time	**stroke** [strok] 打擊、一撞、撫摸 the action of hitting the ball in games; a hit; to touch gently
interpret [ɪnˈtɜprɪt] 說明、解讀、翻譯 to explain; to translate from one language to another	**technological** [tɛknəˈlɑdʒɪkl̩] 技術上的 related to scientific knowledge
interruption [ˌɪntəˈrʌpʃən] 中斷、妨礙 something that interrupts	**terrify** [ˈtɛrəˌfaɪ] 使恐懼、使驚嚇 to make someone extremely afraid
limitation [ˌlɪməˈteʃən] 限制 the fact that being limited	**thorough** [ˈθru] 徹底的 complete
monument [ˈmɑnjəmənt] 紀念碑 a statue or structure built to remind people of an important event or famous person	**witness** [ˈwɪtnɪs] 目擊者、目擊 someone who sees a crime or an accident and can describe what happened

3

◉ 捷徑文化版權所有

◆用中文解釋猜猜英文單字

ACROSS

1 描繪
3 懲罰
6 往返
7 部份的
10 乳液、洗潔劑
12 有鎖的收納櫃、寄物櫃
14 投資額、投資
15 爆炸

DOWN

1 擁有物
2 本能、直覺
4 輸送、運輸工具
5 手寫
8 有可能的、有希望的
9 恢復
11 兇手
13 毀滅

◆上面的遊戲會用到的單字都在這裡！真的看不懂提示就來偷瞄一下吧！

WORD BANK: Explosion, handwriting, instinct, investment, locker, lotion, murderer, partial, penalty, portray, possession, promising, recovery, ruin, shuttle, transportation.

答案就在後面

◆填字遊戲解答在這裡！

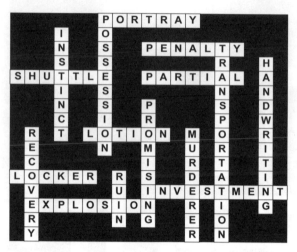

◆單字還記不熟嗎？快來做複習！

explosion [ɪkˋsploʒən]	penalty [ˋpɛnl̩tɪ]
爆炸 such as bomb is made to explode	懲罰 a punishment for breaking a law or legal agreement
handwriting [ˋhænd͵raɪtɪŋ]	portray [porˋtre]
手寫 the way of a person's writing	描繪 to be or make a representation or description of
instinct [ˋɪnstɪŋkt]	possession [pəˋzɛʃən]
本能、直覺 unlearned, to act in a certain way out of human nature	擁有物 the things that you own
investment [ɪnˋvɛstmənt]	promising [ˋprɑmɪsɪŋ]
投資額、投資 the use of money to get a profit	有可能的、有希望的 showing signs of being successful in the future
locker [ˋlɑkɚ]	recovery [rɪˋkʌvərɪ]
有鎖的收納櫃、寄物櫃 a small cupboard with a lock where you can leave your belongings while doing something	恢復 getting better after an illness, injury
lotion [ˋloʃən]	ruin [ˋruɪn]
乳液、清潔劑 a thick liquid that you put on the skin to moisturize it; a think liquid for removing dirt	毀滅 to destroy thoroughly
murderer [ˋmɝdərɚ]	shuttle [ˋʃʌtl̩]
兇手 someone who commits a crime of killing someone	往返 transportation that makes regular short journeys between two places
partial [ˋpɑrʃəl]	transportation [͵trænspɚˋteʃən]
部分的 not complete; only a certain part	輸送、運輸工具 a method for carrying passengers or goods from one place to another

4

◉ 捷徑文化版權所有

◆用中文解釋猜猜英文單字

ACROSS

1 素描、草圖
4 物種
6 停止、使停止
9 無聊的、可厭的
10 明確的
12 裝備、設備
13 細語、抱怨
15 插入

DOWN

2 擴張
3 電報機
5 雪橇
7 移民者
8 專業
11 段落
14 傾斜、倚靠
16 輕打、水龍頭

◆上面的遊戲會用到的單字都在這裡！真的看不懂提示就來偷瞄一下吧！

WORD BANK: Equipment, expansion, halt, immigrant, insert, lean, murmur, paragraph, precise, profession, sketch, sledge, species, tap, telegraph, tiresome.

答案就在後面

◆填字遊戲解答在這裡！

```
      S K E T C H
    T       X
    E     S P E C I E S
  H A L T   A         L
P   E     N   T I R E S O M E
R   G     S         D   M
O   P R E C I S E     G   I       P
F   A     O         E   G       A
E Q U I P M E N T         M U R M U R
S   H               A       A
S   L               N       G
I N S E R T           T       R
O   A   A                   A
N   N   P                   P
                          H
```

◆單字還記不熟嗎？快來做複習！

equipment [ɪˈkwɪpmənt] 裝備、設備 the tools, items, etc. that you require to do a particular activity	**precise** [prɪˈsaɪs] 明確的 exact and accurate
expansion [ɪkˈspænʃən] 擴張 a state when something increases in size or amount	**profession** [prəˈfɛʃən] 專業 a form of employment and that is respected in society as well-trained, knowledgeable, and honorable
halt [hɔlt] 停止、使停止 to stop or pause	**sketch** [skɛtʃ] 素描、草圖 a simple, quickly-made drawing
immigrant [ˈɪməgrənt] 移民者 someone coming into a nation and living in a country from abroad	**sledge** [slɛdʒ] 雪橇 a large open vehicle that is used for travelling over snow and is pulled by animals
insert [ɪnˈsɝt] 插入 to put something into something else	**species** [ˈspiʃɪz] 物種 a distinct kind
lean [lin] 傾斜、倚靠 to bend from an upright position	**tap** [tæp] 輕打、水龍頭 to hit someone or something gently; faucet
murmur [ˈmɝmɚ] 細語、抱怨 a mumbled or muttered complaint	**telegraph** [ˈtɛləˌgræf] 電報機 a device for sending messages by radio or electrical signals
paragraph [ˈpærəˌgræf] 段落 a division of a piece of writing which is made up of one or more sentences and begins a new line	**tiresome** [ˈtaɪrsəm] 無聊的、可厭的 bored, making you feel annoyed

5

◉ 捷徑文化版權所有

◆用中文解釋猜猜英文單字

ACROSS

1 說服
4 知識份子、智力的、聰明的
7 風景
11 農村的
13 捲入、連累
14 羞辱、辱罵
15 減緩

DOWN

1 名望、流行
2 食譜、秘訣
3 基礎、原則
5 顯露、揭發
6 驅策、勸告、極力主張
8 建議
9 以雕刻裝飾、雕塑品
10 容器
12 改進、改革

◆上面的遊戲會用到的單字都在這裡！真的看不懂提示就來偷瞄一下吧！

WORD BANK: Container, exposure, fundamental, insult, intellectual, involvement, landscape, persuasion, popularity, recipe, reform, relieve, rural, sculpture, suggestion, urge.

029

◆填字遊戲解答在這裡！

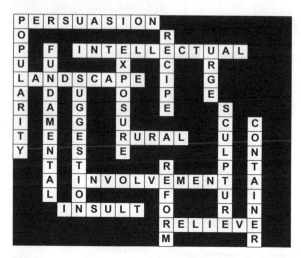

◆單字還記不熟嗎？快來做複習！

container [kənˈtenə] 容器 a box or similar object that you use to keep things in	**popularity** [ˌpɑpjəˈlærəti] 名望、流行 something is liked or supported by a group of people
exposure [ɪkˈspoʒə] 顯露、揭發 the state of being uncovered to something dangerous	**recipe** [ˈrɛsəpi] 食譜、秘訣 a list of instruction for cooking a dish
fundamental [ˌfʌndəˈmɛntl̩] 基礎、原則 a basic and important rule	**reform** [rɪˈfɔrm] 改進、改革 to change your behavior and become a better person, improve
insult [ɪnˈsʌlt] 羞辱、辱罵 to treat or speak to with great disrespect	**relieve** [rɪˈliv] 減緩 to lessen pain, anxiety, or trouble
intellectual [ˌɪntl̩ˈɛktʃuəl] 知識份子、智力的、聰明的 someone with a highly developed knowledge	**rural** [ˈrurəl] 農村的 relating to the country; country life
involvement [ɪnˈvɑlvmənt] 捲入、連累 the process of being a part of something	**sculpture** [ˈskʌlptʃə] 以雕刻裝飾、雕塑品 an object made out of stone, wood, clay etc by artists
landscape [ˈlænskep] 風景 a wide view of a section of nature	**suggestion** [səˈdʒɛstʃən] 建議 an advice you give to someone about what they should do
persuasion [pəˈsweʒən] 說服 the act of persuading someone to do something	**urge** [ɝdʒ] 驅策、勸告、權力主張 to strongly suggest that someone does something

6

◉ 捷徑文化版權所有

◆用中文解釋猜猜英文單字

ACROSS

2 現實的
6 押韻
7 薑
8 磨光、擦亮、潤飾
9 輕視、打噴嚏
13 傲人的、傑出的
14 參加
15 容器、碗、血管、船

DOWN

1 信差
3 忠心的
4 牧師、部長
5 研磨、碾
8 獨特的
10 獲得
11 強烈的、緊張的
12 相互的

◆上面的遊戲會用到的單字都在這裡！真的看不懂提示就來偷瞄一下吧！

WORD BANK: Ginger, grind, intense, loyal, messenger, minister, mutual, obtain, outstanding, participation, peculiar, polish, realistic, rhyme, sneeze, vessel.

031

答案就在後面

Level-2

◆填字遊戲解答在這裡！

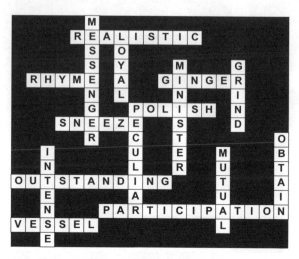

◆單字還記不熟嗎？快來做複習！

ginger [ˈdʒɪndʒɚ] 薑 a hot spice plant used in cooking	**outstanding** [aʊtˈstændɪŋ] 傲人的、傑出的 excellent; distinguished
grind [graɪnd] 研磨、碾 to break something into small pieces	**participation** [parˌtɪsəˈpeʃən] 參加 the act of taking part in an event
intense [ɪnˈtɛns] 強烈的、緊張的 extremely nervous and anxious	**peculiar** [pɪˈkjuljɚ] 獨特的 strange or unusual
loyal [ˈlɔɪəl] 忠心的 faithful, always supporting your friends, country...etc.	**polish** [ˈpɑlɪʃ] 磨光、擦亮、潤飾 to make something smooth, bright and shiny by rubbing it
messenger [ˈmɛsŋdʒɚ] 信差 a person who delivers messages to someone else	**realistic** [rɪəˈlɪstɪk] 現實的 showing realism
minister [ˈmɪnɪstɚ] 牧師、部長 a leader in charge of a government department	**rhyme** [raɪm] 押韻 a short and not serious piece of writing, using words that rhyme
mutual [ˈmjutʃʊəl] 相互的 shared in common	**sneeze** [sniz] 輕視、打噴嚏 to exhale breath from the nose and mouth in a sudden
obtain [əbˈten] 獲得 to acquire something that you want	**vessel** [ˈvɛsl̩] 容器、碗、血管、船 a big boat; a container that holds liquids

7

◉ 捷徑文化版權所有

◆用中文解釋猜猜英文單字

ACROSS

1 清白、天真無邪
4 參考、提及
5 獻祭、犧牲
7 使工業（產業）化
9 粗暴地、粗略地
10 月亮的、陰曆的
12 通貨膨脹、膨脹
13 妨礙
14 觀光、遊覽

DOWN

1 使感染
2 擴大、延長
3 俯瞰
5 薪水
6 惡夢、夢魘
8 屈服、投降
11 啟發、鼓舞

◆上面的遊戲會用到的單字都在這裡！真的看不懂提示就來偷瞄一下吧！

WORD BANK: Expand, industrialize, infect, inflation, innocence, inspire, interfere, lunar, nightmare, overlook, refer, roughly, sacrifice, salary, sightseeing, surrender.

033

答案就在後面

◆填字遊戲解答在這裡！

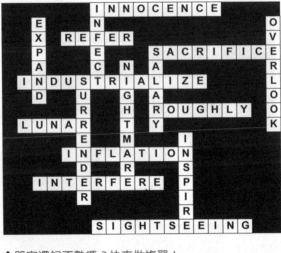

◆單字還記不熟嗎？快來做複習！

expand [ɪkˋspænd] 擴大、延長 to become larger in size, number...etc.	**nightmare** [ˋnaɪtˎmɛr] 惡夢、夢魘 a very frightening dream
industrialize [ɪnˋdʌstrɪəˎlaɪz] 使工業（產業）化 to establish industries in a country	**overlook** [ˎovəˋluk] 俯瞰 to look at from above
infect [ɪnˋfɛkt] 使感染 to pass a disease to someone	**refer** [rɪˋfɝ] 參考、提及 to mention or speak about
inflation [ɪnˋfleʃən] 通貨膨脹、膨脹 the action of a continuing increase in prices	**roughly** [ˋrʌflɪ] 粗暴地、粗略地 in a rough manner; approximately
innocence [ˋɪnəsn̩s] 清白、天真無邪 the state of being innocent	**sacrifice** [ˋsækrəˎfaɪs] 獻祭、犧牲 to forgo something valuable to help others
inspire [ɪnˋspaɪr] 啟發、鼓舞 to encourage someone in the ability to take effective action	**salary** [ˋsælərɪ] 薪水 money, usually paid directly into one's bank account once a month, that one receives as payment from the company or organization one works for
interfere [ˎɪntəˋfɪr] 妨礙 take part in a matter which does not concern one; interrupt	**sightseeing** [ˋsaɪtˎsiɪŋ] 觀光、遊覽 the activity of visiting somewhere
lunar [ˋlunə] 月亮的、陰曆的 relating to the moon	**surrender** [səˋrɛndə] 屈服、投降 to say officially that you want to stop fighting because you understand that you are unable to win; to give in

8

◉ 捷徑文化版權所有

◆用中文解釋猜猜英文單字

ACROSS

1 收回、撤出
5 被動的、消極的
7 扒手
10 降落傘
11 交響樂、交響曲
14 例外
15 位置
16 近視的

DOWN

2 印象、影響
3 革命、改革
4 關於
6 風景、景色
8 毀壞、壓榨
9 拒絕
12 適度的、溫和的
13 反對、抗議

◆上面的遊戲會用到的單字都在這裡！真的看不懂提示就來偷瞄一下吧！

WORD BANK: Crush, exception, impression, location, moderate, nearsighted, parachute, passive, pickpocket, protest, refusal, regarding, revolution, scenery, symphony, withdraw.

答案就在後面

◆填字遊戲解答在這裡！

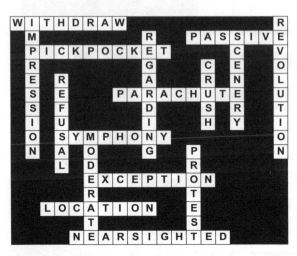

◆單字還記不熟嗎？快來做複習！

crush [krʌʃ]	pickpocket [ˋpɪkˌpɑkɪt]
毀壞、壓榨 to break something with violence	扒手 someone who steals from other's pockets
exception [ɪkˋsɛpʃən]	**protest** [ˋprotɛst]
例外 something that is not included	反對、抗議 an action of showing disapproval or opposition to something
impression [ɪmˋprɛʃən]	**refusal** [rɪˋfjuzl̩]
印象、影響 a feeling on someone at first glance	拒絕 the chance to reject something before it is offered to another
location [loˋkeʃən]	**regarding** [rɪˋgɑrdɪŋ]
位置 a place	關於 about, concerning
moderate [ˋmɑdərɪt]	**revolution** [ˌrɛzəˋluʃən]
適度的、溫和的 mild, average in degree	革命、改革 determination
nearsighted [ˋnɪrˋsaɪtɪd]	**scenery** [ˋsinərɪ]
近視的 only seeing things clearly when they are close	風景、景色 view
parachute [ˋpærəˌʃut]	**symphony** [ˋsɪmfənɪ]
降落傘 a large piece of cloth fastened by thin ropes to people or objects that are dropped from aircraft in order to make them fall slowly	交響樂、交響曲 a long piece of music usually in four parts
passive [ˋpæsɪv]	**withdraw** [wɪðˋdrɔ]
被動的、消極的 someone who is not active to accept what others do	收回、撤出 to stop giving support or taking part in an activity

9

◉ 捷徑文化版權所有

◆用中文解釋猜猜英文單字

ACROSS

1 馬拉松
3 磁性的、有魅力的
5 習慣性的
8 地震、震動
9 吝嗇的
13 語調、吟詠
14 款待、娛樂
15 卑鄙的
16 生命的、不可或缺的

DOWN

2 忽視、忽略
4 宗族的、部落的
6 註冊
7 製造業
10 經濟學
11 令人不快的、冒犯人的
12 金融的、財政的

◆上面的遊戲會用到的單字都在這裡！真的看不懂提示就來偷瞄一下吧！

WORD BANK: Economics, entertainment, financial, habitual, intonation, lousy, magnetic, manufacture, marathon, neglect, offensive, quake, registration, stingy, tribal, vital.

答案就在後面

◆填字遊戲解答在這裡！

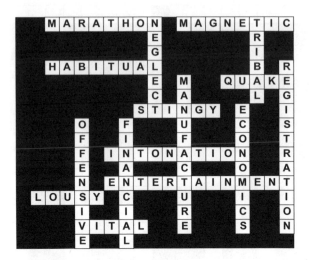

◆單字還記不熟嗎？快來做複習！

economics [ˌikə`nɑmɪks] 經濟學 the study concerned with the production, consumption etc.	**marathon** [`mærəˌθɑn] 馬拉松 a long-distance running race of about 26 miles
entertainment [ˌɛntɚ`tenmənt] 款待、娛樂 the action of being entertained	**neglect** [nɪ`glɛkt] 忽視、忽略 fail to look after or pay little attention to
financial [faɪ`nænʃəl] 金融的、財政的 relating to money	**offensive** [ə`fɛnsɪv] 令人不快的、冒犯人的 rude or insulting and likely to cause anger
habitual [hə`bɪtʃʊəl] 習慣性的 done as a habit	**quake** [kwek] 地震、震動 to shake or tremble
intonation [ˌɪnto`neʃən] 語調、吟詠 rise and fall in the level of the voice	**registration** [ˌrɛdʒɪ`streʃən] 註冊 the act of registering
lousy [`lauzɪ] 卑鄙的 awful, terrible	**stingy** [`stɪndʒɪ] 吝嗇的 not generous especially with money
magnetic [mæg`nɛtɪk] 磁性的、有魅力的 having the power of a magnet; charming	**tribal** [traɪbl̩] 宗族的、部落的 relating to with a tribe
manufacture [ˌmænjə`fæktʃɚ] 製造業 the process of making goods or materials using machines	**vital** [`vaɪtl̩] 生命的、不可或缺的 very important and necessary for something to exist; essential

10

◉ 捷徑文化版權所有

◆用中文解釋猜猜英文單字

ACROSS

2 便利
6 孤立、隔離
7 探查、探險
8 可疑的
10 大部份地
12 打字員
14 年少的
15 管弦樂隊
16 指關節

DOWN

1 果斷、決心
3 客觀的、目標
4 滿足
5 公式、法則、嬰兒奶粉
9 精神的、心靈的
11 遇險、摧毀、毀壞
13 辛辣的、加香料的

◆上面的遊戲會用到的單字都在這裡！真的看不懂提示就來偷瞄一下吧！

WORD BANK: Convenience, explore, formula, isolate, junior, knuckle, largely, objective, orchestra, resolution, satisfaction, spicy, spiritual, suspicious, typist, wreck.

答案就在後面

◆填字遊戲解答在這裡！

◆單字還記不熟嗎？快來做複習！

convenience [kən`vinjəns] 便利 the quality of being useful especially by making something easier and saving your time	**orchestra** [`ɔrkɪstrə] 管弦樂隊 a group of musicians playing many different kinds of instruments
explore [ɪk`splor] 探查、探險 to travel around an unfamiliar area in order to find out about it	**resolution** [ˌrɛzə`luʃən] 果斷、決心 determination
formula [`fɔrmjələ] 公式、法則、嬰兒奶粉 a set of principles that you use to solve a problem; a liquid food for infants, containing most of the nutrients in human milk	**satisfaction** [ˌsætɪs`fækʃən] 滿足 the state of happiness or pleasure, fulfillment
isolate [`aɪsˌet] 孤立、隔離 to keep apart from others	**spicy** [`spaɪsɪ] 辛辣的、加香料的 strongly flavored with spice
junior [`dʒunjɚ] 年少的 younger; someone who is younger	**spiritual** [`spɪrɪtʃʊəl] 精神的、心靈的 relating to spirit rather than to material things
knuckle [`nʌkḷ] 指關節 a finger joint esp. the joint connecting a finger to the hand	**suspicious** [sə`spɪʃəs] 可疑的 feeling doubtful about something or someone
largely [`lɑrdʒlɪ] 大部分地 for the most part; on a large scale	**typist** [`taɪpɪst] 打字員 someone whose job is typing
objective [əb`dʒɛktɪv] 客觀的、目標 being not influenced by others; goal	**wreck** [rɛk] 遇險、摧毀、毀壞 a car, plane or train that has been damaged badly

11

◆用中文解釋猜猜英文單字

ACROSS	DOWN
3 鋼琴師	**1** 同情
5 造反者、反抗者	**2** 皺紋
9 追求	**4** 悲劇
12 保存、維護	**6** 衝浪
13 忠實的、耿直的、可靠的	**7** 拔河
14 羞怯的	**8** 重複
15 簽名	**10** 放鬆
16 急迫的、緊急的	**11** 香水

◆上面的遊戲會用到的單字都在這裡！真的看不懂提示就來偷瞄一下吧！

WORD BANK: Faithful, perfume, pianist, preserve, pursuit, rebel, relaxation, repetition, signature, surf, sympathy, timid, tragedy, tug-of-war, urgent, wrinkle.

答案就在後面

◆填字遊戲解答在這裡！

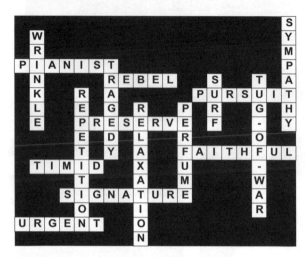

◆單字還記不熟嗎？快來做複習！

faithful [ˈfɛθfəl] 忠實的、耿直的、可靠的 loyal and trustworthy	**signature** [ˈsɪgnətʃə] 簽名 a person's name written in a typical way
perfume [ˈpɝfjum] 香水 a sweet or pleasant smell	**surf** [sɝf] 衝浪 to ride on waves while standing on a special board
pianist [pɪˈænɪst] 鋼琴師 a person who plays the piano	**sympathy** [ˈsɪmpəθɪ] 同情 the feeling of being sorry for someone who is in a bad situation
preserve [prɪˈzɝv] 保存、維護 to save something from being destroyed	**tragedy** [ˈtrædʒədɪ] 悲劇 something very bad that happens
pursuit [pɚˈsut] 追求 someone who tries to achieve something in a strong way	**timid** [ˈtɪmɪd] 羞怯的 shy; lack of confidence
rebel [ˈrɛbl̩] 造反者、反抗者 someone who fights against people in authority	**tug-of-war** [tʌg əv wɔr] 拔河 a contest in which two teams pull opposite ends of a rope against each other
relaxation [ˌrilæksˈeʃən] 放鬆 ease	**urgent** [ˈɝdʒənt] 急迫的、緊急的 needing very immediate action
repetition [ˌrɛpɪˈtɪʃən] 重複 the act of repeating, or something repeated	**wrinkle** [ˈrɪŋkl̩] 皺紋 lines are on your face and skin when you get old

12

◉ 捷徑文化版權所有

◆用中文解釋猜猜英文單字

ACROSS

3 背誦
4 障礙物、妨礙
6 回收、循環利用
9 山崩
12 素食主義者
13 音節
14 二年級學生
16 引用

DOWN

1 教授
2 類似
5 輝煌的、閃耀的
7 儘管如此、然而
8 抵抗
10 安裝、裝置
11 令人欣喜的
15 陰謀、情節

◆上面的遊戲會用到的單字都在這裡！真的看不懂提示就來偷瞄一下吧！

WORD BANK: Delightful, install, landslide,
nevertheless, obstacle, plot, professor, quotation,
recite, recycle, resemble, resistance, sophomore,
splendid, syllable, vegetarian.

Level-2

◆填字遊戲解答在這裡！

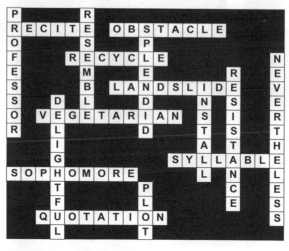

◆單字還記不熟嗎？快來做複習！

delightful [dɪˋlaɪt] 令人欣喜的 very joyful	**recite** [rɪˋsaɪt] 背誦 to read out aloud from memory like a poem, a piece of literature before viewers
install [ɪnˋstɔl] 安裝、裝置 to put something in position or set it up	**recycle** [riˋsaɪkl̩] 回收、循環利用 to use again
landslide [ˋlænd͵slaɪd] 山崩 a sudden fall of rocks and earth down a hill, cliff etc.	**resemble** [rɪˋzɛmbl̩] 類似 to be similar to something or someone
nevertheless [͵nɛvɚðəˋlɛs] 儘管如此、然而 however, although	**resistance** [rɪˋzɪstəns] 抵抗 an act of resisting
obstacle [ˋɑbstəkl̩] 障礙物、妨礙 a thing that blocks one's way	**sophomore** [ˋsɑfə͵mor] 二年級學生 a second-year college student
plot [plɑt] 陰謀、情節 a secret plan to do something harmful; the main storyline of a tale	**splendid** [ˋsplɛndɪd] 輝煌的、閃耀的 beautiful and impressive; magnificent
professor [prəˋfɛsɚ] 教授 a teacher of the highest rank in a university department	**syllable** [ˋsɪləbl̩] 音節 a word or part of a word which contains a single vowel sound
quotation [kwoˋteʃən] 引用 a sentence or phrase from a book reiterated by someone other than the originator	**vegetarian** [͵vɛdʒəˋtɛrɪən] 素食主義者 a person who only eats vegetables

13

◉ 捷徑文化版權所有

◆用中文解釋猜猜英文單字

ACROSS

1 清爽、茶點
4 並且、此外
5 路線
6 麻雀
9 推銷員
10 知識
12 當今、現在
14 月刊、每個月的

DOWN

1 限制
2 僅僅、不過
3 評論、批評
7 廢棄、拒絕
8 重聚、團圓
9 抓
11 橢圓形
13 愛滋病

◆上面的遊戲會用到的單字都在這裡！真的看不懂提示就來偷瞄一下吧！

WORD BANK: Aids, criticism, information, mere, monthly, moreover, nowadays, oval, refreshment, rejection, restriction, reunion, route, salesperson, scratch, sparrow.

答案就在後面

◆填字遊戲解答在這裡！

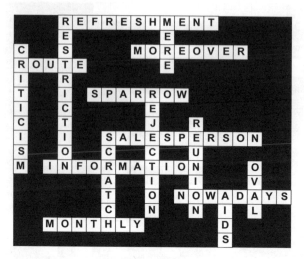

◆單字還記不熟嗎？快來做複習！

AIDS [edz] 愛滋病 a serious disease that destroys your body from defending itself against infection, and causes death usually	**refreshment** [rɪˋfrɛʃmənt] 清爽、茶點 the state of being refreshed
criticism [ˋkrɪtəˌsɪzəm] 評論、批評 expression of disapproval	**rejection** [rɪˋdʒɛkʃən] 廢棄、拒絕 the act of not accepting or agreeing with something
information [ˌɪnfɚˋmeʃən] 知識 facts about a person or situation	**restriction** [rɪˋstrɪkʃən] 限制 the act of restricting, or something that restricts
mere [mɪr] 僅僅、不過 only; just	**reunion** [riˋjunjən] 重聚、團圓 a meeting of friends or fellow-workers after a separation
monthly [ˋmʌnθlɪ] 月刊、每個月的 once a month	**route** [rut] 路線 a way or direction from one place to another
moreover [morˋovɚ] 並且、此外 besides, furthermore	**salesperson** [ˋselzˌpɚsn̩] 推銷員 a sales representative
nowadays [ˋnauəˌdez] 當今、現在 in recent days; now	**scratch** [skrætʃ] 抓 to make a mark on or a small wound in by rubbing with something pointed or rough
oval [ˋovl̩] 橢圓形 egg-shaped	**sparrow** [ˋspæro] 麻雀 a small brown bird

◆用中文解釋猜猜英文單字

ACROSS

2 作用、操作、手術
4 觀察力
7 名譽、聲望
8 髒亂的
11 聚集、集合
13 作曲家、作家
14 無意義的、徒然的
15 變亮、減輕

DOWN

1 標語、口號
3 預測
5 教導、指令
6 頭戴式耳機
8 胡鬧、危害
9 保持
10 妨害、違反
12 泥濘的

◆上面的遊戲會用到的單字都在這裡！真的看不懂提示就來偷瞄一下吧！

WORD BANK: Assemble, composer, headphone, instruct, lighten, messy, mischief, muddy, observation, operation, predict, reputation, retain, slogan, vain, violate.

答案就在後面

◆填字遊戲解答在這裡！

◆單字還記不熟嗎？快來做複習！

assemble [əˈsɛmblɪ] 聚集、集合 a group of persons gathered together for a general purpose	**observation** [ˌɑbzɚˈveʃən] 觀察力 the process of watching someone or something carefully
composer [kəmˈpozɚ] 作曲家、作家 someone who composes music or writes articles	**operation** [ˌɑpəˈreʃən] 作用、操作、手術 the condition or process of working
headphone [ˈhɛdˌfon(z)] 頭戴式耳機 a piece of equipment that you wear over your ears to listen to the music	**predict** [prɪˈdɪkt] 預測 to see or describe in advance as a result of knowledge, experience, or thought
instruct [ɪnˈstrʌkt] 教導、指令 to teach or show someone what to do	**reputation** [ˌrɛpjəˈteʃən] 名譽、聲望 estimation in which someone or something is commonly held
lighten [ˈlaɪtn̩] 變亮、減輕 become brighter or less heavy	**retain** [rɪˈten] 保持 maintain
messy [ˈmɛsɪ] 髒亂的 untidy or not clean	**slogan** [ˈsloɡən] 標語、口號 a short phrase which is easy to be remembered and usually used in advertisements
mischief [ˈmɪstʃɪf] 胡鬧、危害 bad behavior, especially by children that cause no serious harm	**vain** [ven] 無意義的、徒然的 without purpose or positive results
muddy [ˈmʌdɪ] 泥濘的 containing mud; full of mud	**violate** [ˈvaɪəˌlet] 妨害、違反 to disobey or do something against a law

15

◉ 捷徑文化版權所有

◆用中文解釋猜猜英文單字

ACROSS

2 直升機
4 同輩
6 電機工程學
10 偶像
11 骨架、體制
13 習慣、習俗、使用
14 地點、位置
15 即、就是
16 代表、表示、表現

DOWN

1 使恢復精神
3 實驗室
5 百分率
7 成份、原料（複數）
8 誠懇、真摯
9 估計、評價
12 使彎曲

◆上面的遊戲會用到的單字都在這裡！真的看不懂提示就來偷瞄一下吧！

WORD BANK: Curve, electronics, evaluate, frame, helicopter, idol, ingredients, laboratory, namely, peer, percentage, refresh, representation, sincerity, site, usage.

答案就在後面

Level-2

◆填字遊戲解答在這裡！

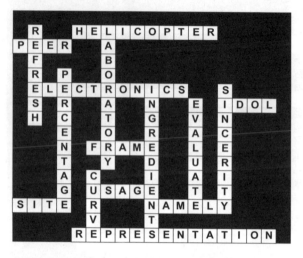

◆單字還記不熟嗎？快來做複習！

curve [kɝv] 使彎曲 a line that bends like part of a circle	**namely** [ˋnemlɪ] 即、就是 that is to say
electronics [ɪlɛkˋtrɑnɪks] 電子學 the study concerned with the design of circuits and the behavior of electrons	**peer** [pɪr] 同輩 a person who is the same age or the same rank
evaluate [ɪˋvæljuˏet] 估計、評價 to judge the value or worth of someone or something	**percentage** [pɚˋsɛntɪdʒ] 百分率 a given part in every hundred
frame [frem] 骨架、體制 a firm border or case into which holds something in place	**refresh** [rɪˋfrɛʃ] 使恢復精神 to give new energy to feel great and less tired
helicopter [ˋhɛlɪˏkɑptɚ] 直升機 a type of aircraft with large blades on top which turn around fast	**representation** [ˏrɛprɪzɛnˋteʃən] 代表、表示、表現 the act of representing or state of being represented
idol [ˋaɪdḷ] 偶像 someone you admire very much	**sincerity** [sɪnˋsɛrətɪ] 誠懇、真摯 open heartedness, when someone really means something
ingredients [ɪnˋgridɪəntz] 成份、原料 any of the things that are used to make a particular dish	**site** [saɪt] 地點、位置 an area of ground where something is being built or will be built
laboratory [ˋlæbrəˏtorɪ] 實驗室 a room for scientific experiments	**usage** [ˋjusɪdʒ] 習慣、習俗、使用 the way in which something is used

16

◉ 捷徑文化版權所有

◆用中文解釋猜猜英文單字

ACROSS

1 巨大的、廣大的
5 輸入
6 恢復
8 發表、出版
10 搭救
12 青年旅舍
13 技師、技術員
14 衛星
15 增進、促銷、升遷

DOWN

2 紀念品
3 專業的
4 慈悲
7 心理學
8 豐富的
9 強度、強烈
11 電報

◆上面的遊戲會用到的單字都在這裡！真的看不懂提示就來偷瞄一下吧！

WORD BANK: Hostel, input, intensity, mercy, plentiful, professional, promotion, psychology, publication, rescue, restore, satellite, souvenir, technician, telegram, vast.

051

答案就在後面

◆填字遊戲解答在這裡！

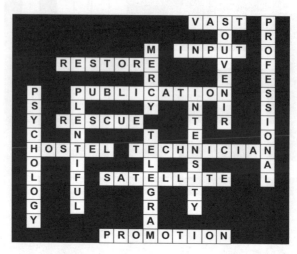

◆單字還記不熟嗎？快來做複習！

hostel [ˈhɑstl̩] 青年旅舍 a house which provides cheap rooms, food for people to stay	**publication** [ˌpʌblɪˈkeʃən] 發表、出版 the act of making something known to the public
input [ˈɪnˌpʊt] 輸入 the act of putting in	**rescue** [ˈrɛskju] 搭救 to save someone from a danger or harm
intensity [ɪnˈtɛnsəti] 強度、強烈 the state of being intense; extreme	**restore** [rɪˈstor] 恢復 to return something or someone to a previous condition
mercy [ˈmɝsi] 慈悲 kindness; compassion	**satellite** [ˈsætl̩ˌaɪt] 衛星 a body in space that moves around a larger one, esp. a planet
plentiful [ˈplɛntɪfəl] 豐富的 more than enough in quantity	**souvenir** [ˌsuvəˈnɪr] 紀念品 a thing that you buy to remind yourself of a special occasion
professional [prəˈfɛʃənl̩] 專業的 someone who works in a particular field; performing a job to high standards	**technician** [tɛkˈnɪʃən] 技師、技術員 someone whose job is to check machines or equipment and make sure they are working properly
promotion [prəˈmoʃən] 增進、促銷、升遷 advancement in rank or position	**telegram** [ˈtɛləˌgræm] 電報 a message delivered by telegraph
psychology [saɪˈkɑlədʒɪ] 心理學 the study or science of the mind and the way it works and influences behavior	**vast** [væst] 巨大的、廣大的 very big or giant

17

◉ 捷徑文化版權所有

◆用中文解釋猜猜英文單字

ACROSS

3 表示同情的
4 上傳（檔案）
8 軟體
9 花瓣
11 最小量、最低速、最低限度
13 網站
14 器官的、有機的
15 凹處、插座

DOWN

1 小圓石、鵝卵石
2 海盜
5 使不愉快、使憤怒、冒犯
6 分詞
7 相同的
8 劈開、分化
10 宣傳、出風頭
12 動詞

◆上面的遊戲會用到的單字都在這裡！真的看不懂提示就來偷瞄一下吧！

WORD BANK: Identical, minimum, offend, organic, participle, pebble, petal, pirate, publicity, socket, software, split, sympathetic, upload, verb, website.

答案就在後面

◆填字遊戲解答在這裡！

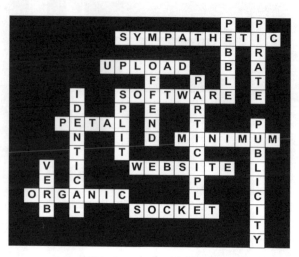

◆單字還記不熟嗎？快來做複習！

identical [aɪˋdɛntɪkl̩] 相同的 very same or equal	**publicity** [pʌbˋlɪsətɪ] 宣傳、出風頭 the attention that someone gets from the media for instance TV, newspapers, magazines, etc.
minimum [ˋmɪnəməm] 最小量、最低速、最低限度 the smallest amount of something	**socket** [ˋsɑkɪt] 凹處、插座 a hollow piece or part into which something fits
offend [əˋfɛnd] 使不愉快、使憤怒、冒犯 to hurt the feelings of	**software** [ˋsɔftˌwɛr] 軟體 programs used by a computer
organic [ɔrˋgænɪk] 器官的、有機的 relating to the organs of the body	**split** [splɪt] 劈開、分化 to separate into parts
participle [ˋpɑrtəsəpl̩] 分詞 a non-finite verb form that can be used in compound forms of the verb or as an adjective	**sympathetic** [ˌsɪmpəˋθɛtɪk] 表示同情的 feeling sorry about someone's problem
pebble [ˋpɛbl̩] 小圓石、鵝卵石 a small smooth stone found especially on a beach	**upload** [ʌpˋlod] 上傳（檔案） to transfer or move a computer program or data to a larger computer network
petal [ˋpɛtl̩] 花瓣 any of the usually colored leaf like divisions of a flower	**verb** [vɝb] 動詞 a word which is used to describe an action
pirate [ˋpaɪrət] 海盜 a person who sails around stopping and robbing ships at sea	**website** [ˋwɛbˌsaɪt] 網站 a place where you can find information on the Internet

18

◉ 捷徑文化版權所有

◆用中文解釋猜猜英文單字

ACROSS

3 總結、概述
7 首要的、全盛時期、一流的
8 必然的、隨之引起的
10 尼龍
11 神祕的
13 處女
14 反對、反抗
15 殖民者

DOWN

1 唯一的、獨特的
2 放牧、使成群
3 運動員
4 翻譯
5 矛、魚叉
6 軌道
9 服裝、服飾
12 溫和的

◆上面的遊戲會用到的單字都在這裡！真的看不懂提示就來偷瞄一下吧！

WORD BANK: Consequent, costume, counter, herd, mild, mysterious, nylon, orbit, prime, settler, spear, sportsman, summarize, translate, unique, virgin.

答案就在後面

◆填字遊戲解答在這裡！

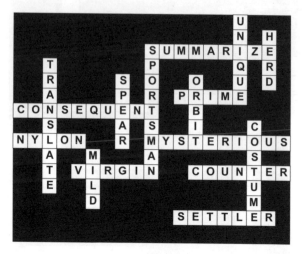

◆單字還記不熟嗎？快來做複習！

consequent [ˈkɑnsəˌkwɛnt]	**prime** [praɪm]
必然的、隨之引起的 happening as a result of something	首要的、全盛時期、一流的 chief
costume [ˈkɑstjum] 服裝、服飾 clothes that are typical of a particular place or period of time in the past	**settler** [ˈsɛtlɚ] 殖民者 a person who settles in an area
counter [ˈkaʊntɚ] 櫃檯 a place where you pay or are served in a shop	**spear** [spɪr] 矛、魚叉 a weapon with a sharp pointed blade used for throwing fish
herd [hɝd] 放牧、使成群 a large number of cattle, sheep or other animals living	**sportsman** [ˈsportsmən] 運動員 someone who plays sports
mild [maɪld] 溫和的 gentle and not severe	**summarize** [ˈsʌməˌraɪz] 總結、概述 to sum up
mysterious [mɪsˈtɪrɪəs] 神祕的 used when situations are difficult to explain or understand	**translate** [trænsˈlet] 翻譯 to express an article in another language
nylon [ˈnaɪlɑn] 尼龍 a strong artificial material that is used to make plastics or clothes	**unique** [juˈnik] 唯一的、獨特的 only one; special
orbit [ˈɔrbɪt] 軌道 to follow the path around the planet; the path through which things in space move around a planet or star	**virgin** [ˈvɝdʒɪn] 處女 someone who has never had sexual experience

19

◉ 捷徑文化版權所有

◆用中文解釋猜猜英文單字

ACROSS

1 悠閒地
6 外科醫生
9 太陽的
10 優點
13 變換
14 謙虛的
15 擴大
16 牽涉、包括

DOWN

2 勞動
3 贈送、呈現
4 螺絲起子
5 保險
7 大學
8 說明、解釋
11 責罵
12 灣、海灣

◆上面的遊戲會用到的單字都在這裡！真的看不懂提示就來偷瞄一下吧！

WORD BANK: Enlarge, explanation, gulf, insurance, involve, labor, leisurely, merit, modest, presentation, scold, screwdriver, shift, solar, surgeon, university.

答案就在後面

◆填字遊戲解答在這裡！

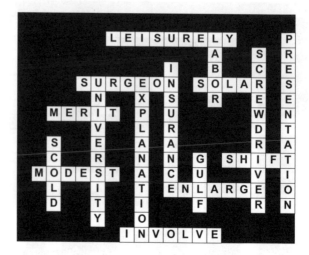

◆單字還記不熟嗎？快來做複習！

enlarge [ɪnˋlɑrdʒ] 擴大 to make something become bigger	**merit** [ˋmɛrɪt] 優點 goodness, worth, value
explanation [ˏɛkspləˋneʃən] 說明、解釋 the reasons you give for why something happened	**presentation** [ˏprɛznˋteʃən] 贈送、呈現 the act of presenting something
gulf [gʌlf] 灣、海灣 a large area of the sea almost enclosed by land	**scold** [skold] 責罵 to angrily criticize someone
insurance [ɪnˋʃurəns] 保險 the business of providing insurance	**screwdriver** [ˋskruˏdraɪvɚ] 螺絲起子 a tool with a narrow blade at one end which fits into the hole cut in the top of a screw for turning it into and out of its place
involve [ɪnˋvɑlv] 牽涉、包括 to cause oneself to become connected	**shift** [ʃɪft] 變換 to move from one position to another; to change
labor [ˋlebɚ] 勞動 workers who work with physical and mental effort	**solar** [ˋsolɚ] 太陽的 relating to the sun
leisurely [ˋliʒɚlɪ] 悠閒地 very relaxed without hurrying	**surgeon** [ˋsɝdʒən] 外科醫生 a doctor who does operations in a hospital
modest [ˋmɑdɪst] 謙虛的 humble, not talking one's abilities or achievements	**university** [ˏjunəˋvɝsətɪ] 大學 an educational institution at the highest level, where students study for a degree

20

◉ 捷徑文化版權所有

◆用中文解釋猜猜英文單字

ACROSS

2 徹夜的、過夜的
4 修正、校訂
5 複數
6 隱私
12 地下道
13 病毒
14 最大的、最高速、最大極度
15 貞操、美德
16 巨大的、極好的

DOWN

1 望遠鏡
3 國籍、國民
7 回憶起、恢復
8 （內科）醫師
9 邏輯
10 鬍子
11 反射、反省、反映

◆上面的遊戲會用到的單字都在這裡！真的看不懂提示就來偷瞄一下吧！

WORD BANK: Logic, maximum, mustache, nationalities, overnight, physician, plural, privacy, recall, reflect, revise, telescope, tremendous, underpass, virtue, virus.

答案就在後面

◆填字遊戲解答在這裡！

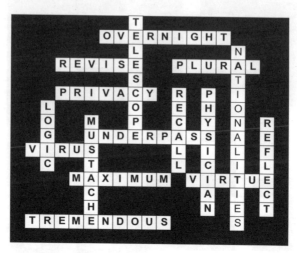

◆單字還記不熟嗎？快來做複習！

logic [ˈlɑdʒɪk] 邏輯 a way of reasonable thinking	**recall** [rɪˈkɔl] 回憶起、恢復 to remember a particular fact from the past
maximum [ˈmæksəməm] 最大的、最高速、最大限度 the largest amount or number	**reflect** [rɪˈflɛkt] 反射、反省、反映 to throw back heat, light, sound, or an image
mustache [ˈmʌstæʃ] 鬍子 hair which grows on a man's upper lip	**revise** [rɪˈvaɪz] 修正、校訂 to alter and improve text or writing
nationality [ˌnæʃənˈæləti] 國籍、國民 the state of being a legal citizen of a particular country	**telescope** [ˈtɛləˌskop] 望遠鏡 an equipment used for making distant objects look closer and larger
overnight [ˈovəˈnaɪt] 徹夜的、過夜的 for during the night	**tremendous** [trɪˈmɛndəs] 巨大的、極好的 extremely good; enormous
physician [fəˈzɪʃən] （內科）醫師 a doctor, especially one who treats diseases with medicines	**underpass** [ˈʌndəˌpæs] 地下道 a road for people to pass under another road or a railway
plural [ˈplurəl] 複數 more than one	**virtue** [ˈvɝtʃu] 貞操、美德 moral goodness of behavior
privacy [ˈpraɪvəsi] 隱私 the state of being free from public attention or able to be alone	**virus** [ˈvaɪrəs] 病毒 a very tiny living thing that causes infection illnesses

21

● 捷徑文化版權所有

◆用中文解釋猜猜英文單字

ACROSS

2 調整、法規
4 即時的
6 進行、著手
7 起源、莖（植物）
9 開始的
12 借貸、借出的東西
13 深思的、思考的、體貼的
14 口琴

DOWN

1 創立者
3 墳墓、葬身之處
4 生產的、多產的
5 發音
6 悲觀的
8 報復
10 義大利麵
11 手工的

◆上面的遊戲會用到的單字都在這裡！真的看不懂提示就來偷瞄一下吧！

WORD BANK: Founder, harmonica, initial, loan, manual, pasta, pessimistic, proceed, productive, prompt, pronunciation, regulation, revenge, stem, thoughtful, tomb.

061

答案就在後面

◆填字遊戲解答在這裡！

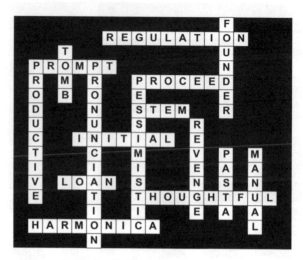

◆單字還記不熟嗎？快來做複習！

founder [ˈfaʊndɚ] 創立者 someone who establishes an organization or an institution	**productive** [prəˈdʌktɪv] 生產的、多產的 producing a large amounts of goods, crops
harmonica [harˈmɑnɪkə] 口琴 a small musical instrument that you play by blowing it from side to side near your	**prompt** [prɑmpt] 即時的 done quickly
initial [ɪˈnɪʃəl] 開始的 happening at the beginning	**pronunciation** [prəˌnʌnsɪˈeʃən] 發音 the way in which a language or a particular word is pronounced
loan [lon] 借貸、借出的東西 something lent especially a sum of money lent	**regulation** [ˌrɛɡjəˈleʃən] 調整、法規 an official rule or order
manual [ˈmænjʊəl] 手工的 a book that gives instructions about how to do something especially how to use a machine	**revenge** [rɪˈvɛndʒ] 報復 punishment given to someone in return for harm done to oneself
pasta [ˈpɑstə] 義大利麵 food made, in various different shapes, from flour paste, and often covered with sauce and cheese	**stem** [stɛm] 起源、莖（植物） the long thin part of a plant
pessimistic [ˌpɛsəˈmɪstɪk] 悲觀的 expecting the worst	**thoughtful** [ˈθɔtfəl] 深思的、思考的、體貼的 thinking very carefully
proceed [prəˈsid] 進行、著手 to begin or continue in a course of action or set of actions	**tomb** [tum] 墳墓、葬身之處 a stone structure above or below the ground where a person is buried after he dies

22

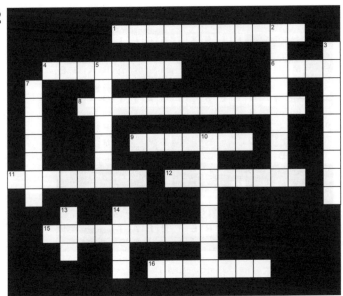

◉ 捷徑文化版權所有

◆用中文解釋猜猜英文單字

ACROSS

1 辨別、分辨
4 複數的、多數的
6 狂怒
8 調查
9 先驅、開拓者
11 傾向、趨向
12 勉強地、幾乎不
15 會議、慣例
16 撤退

DOWN

2 哀痛的、悲傷的
3 減少
5 拉緊、緊張局勢
7 勉強地、幾乎不
10 主考官、審查員
13 收割
14 齒輪

◆上面的遊戲會用到的單字都在這裡！真的看不懂提示就來偷瞄一下吧！

WORD BANK: Convention, distinguish, examiner, gear, investigation, mow, multiple, pioneer, rage, reduction, retreat, scarcely, shelter, sorrowful, tendency, tension.

Level-2

◆填字遊戲解答在這裡！

```
              D I S T I N G U I S H
                            O       R
        M U L T I P L E     R A G E E
      S             E       R       D
      H       I N V E S T I G A T I O N
      E       S             O       U
      L       I     P I O N E E R   C
      T       O     X       F       T
    T E N D E N C Y   S C A R C E L Y I
      R             M       U       O
        M       G   I               N
      C O N V E N T I O N
        W       A   N
                R   R E T R E A T
```

◆單字還記不熟嗎？快來做複習！

convention [kən'vɛnʃən] 會議、慣例 a large formal meeting for people who have the same benefits	**rage** [redʒ] 狂怒 a strong feeling of uncontrollable anger
distinguish [dɪ'stɪŋgwɪʃ] 辨別、分辨 to tell the difference	**reduction** [rɪ'dʌkʃən] 減少 making or becoming less in number
examiner [ɪg'zæmɪnɚ] 主考官、審查員 someone who tests students' knowledge or ability	**retreat** [rɪ'trit] 撤退 to withdraw from the enemy after being defeated in battle
gear [gɪr] 齒輪 a toothed wheel that allows power to be passed from one part of a machine to another so as to control the direction or speed of movement	**scarcely** ['skɛrslɪ] 勉強地、幾乎不 hardly
investigation [ɪnˌvɛstə'geʃən] 調查 a careful search or examination in order to find out more information about	**shelter** ['ʃɛltɚ] 避難所、庇護所 a place giving protection from danger
mow [mo] 收割 to cut down grain or standing grass	**sorrowful** ['sɑrəfəl] 哀痛的、悲傷的 very sad
multiple ['mʌltəpl̩] 複數的、多數的 consisting of many parts, more than one or once	**tendency** ['tɛndənsɪ] 傾向、趨向 a general development in a particular direction or trend
pioneer [ˌpaɪə'nɪr] 先驅、開拓者 a person who goes before, preparing the way for others	**tension** ['tɛnʃən] 拉緊、緊張局勢 tightness or stiffness

23

◉ 捷徑文化版權所有

◆用中文解釋猜猜英文單字

ACROSS

2 懷孕
6 傳奇
8 合法的、守法的
10 說明、插圖
11 聳肩
14 廢話、無意義的話
15 健康、幸福、福利
16 人類、人道

DOWN

1 通貨膨脹、脹大
3 登記、註冊
4 調查員
5 奢侈品、奢侈
7 認知、承認、認出
9 諮詢者、顧問
12 注意、言論、評論
13 夫人、女士

◆上面的遊戲會用到的單字都在這裡！真的看不懂提示就來偷瞄一下吧！

WORD BANK: Consultant, humanity, illustration, inflation, lawful, legend, luxury, madam, nonsense, pregnancy, recognition, register, researcher, remark, shrug, welfare.

答案就在後面

◆填字遊戲解答在這裡！

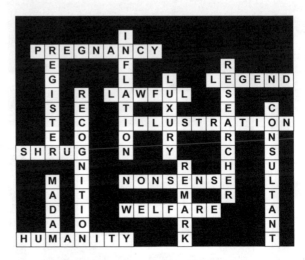

◆單字還記不熟嗎？快來做複習！

consultant [kən'sʌltənt] 諮詢者、顧問 someone who gives advice professionally	**nonsense** ['nɑnsɛns] 廢話、無意義的話 rubbish, opinions that seem very stupid
humanity [hju'mænətɪ] 人類、人道 human qualities, human nature	**pregnancy** ['prɛgnənsɪ] 懷孕 the period or the state of being pregnant
illustration [ɪˌlʌs'treʃən] 說明、插圖 a picture in a book that helps you to understand it	**recognition** [ˌrɛkəg'nɪʃən] 認知、承認、認出 the fact of knowing someone or something
inflation [ɪn'fleʃən] 通貨膨脹、膨大 the state of a continuing increase in prices	**register** ['rɛdʒɪstɚ] 登記、註冊 an official record or list
lawful ['lɔfəl] 合法的、守法的 recognized by law or rules, legal	**researcher** [ri'sɝtʃɚ] 調查員 a person who does research
legend ['lɛdʒənd] 傳奇 an old story about great events and people from ancient times	**remark** [rɪ'mɑrk] 注意、言論、評論 to refer that someone or something is noticed
luxury ['lʌkʃərɪ] 奢侈品、奢侈 great comfort and satisfaction such as you get from the most costly things	**shrug** [ʃrʌg] 聳肩 to raise one's shoulder slightly to show mistrust
madam ['mædəm] 夫人、女士 a polite and respect way of addressing a woman	**welfare** ['wɛlfɛr] 健康、幸福、福利 benefit; happiness

24

◉ 捷徑文化版權所有

◆用中文解釋猜猜英文單字

ACROSS

2 有禮的
5 麻煩的、困難的
9 治療
10 代名詞
11 駭懼、恐怖
14 路標、里程碑
15 理髮師
16 永久的

DOWN

1 棉被
3 諺語
4 否則、要不然
6 戀愛、愛情小說
7 前夕
8 環境、周圍
12 都市的
13 節省、空間的、多餘的

◆上面的遊戲會用到的單字都在這裡！真的看不懂提示就來偷瞄一下吧！

WORD BANK: Eve, landmark, otherwise, permanent, pronoun, proverb, quilt, remedy, respectful, romance, shaver, spare, surrounding, terror, troublesome, urban.

答案就在後面

Level-2

◆填字遊戲解答在這裡！

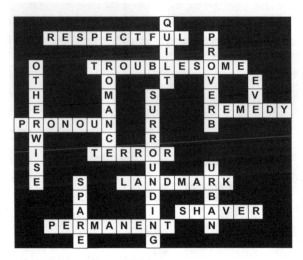

◆單字還記不熟嗎？快來做複習！

eve [iv] 前夕 the day before an important event	**respectful** [rɪ`spɛktfəl] 有禮的 feeling or showing respect
landmark [`lænd͵mɑrk] 路標、里程碑 a sign of a place that is easily seen from a distance	**romance** [ro`mæns] 戀愛、愛情小說 a love affair
otherwise [`ʌðɚ͵waɪz] 否則、要不然 or else; differently; or	**shaver** [`ʃevɚ] 理髮師 someone whose job is to cut or style others' hair
permanent [`pɝmənənt] 永久的 lasting or intending to last for a long time	**spare** [spɛr] 節省、空間的、多餘的 extra
pronoun [`pronaʊn] 代名詞 a word that is used in place of a noun or a noun phrase such as he instead of "Peter" or instead of "the man"	**surrounding** [sə`raʊndɪŋ] 環境、周圍 the place where someone or something is around
proverb [`prɑvɝb] 諺語 a short well-known saying that expresses something that is generally true	**terror** [`tɛrɚ] 駭懼、恐怖 a feeling of fear and fright
quilt [kwɪlt] 棉被 a cloth cover for a bed filled with soft warm material with stitching across it	**troublesome** [`trʌbl̩səm] 麻煩的、困難的 causing problems
remedy [`rɛmədɪ] 治療 a way of curing something	**urban** [`ɝbən] 都市的 relating to towns or cities

25

◉ 捷徑文化版權所有

◆用中文解釋猜猜英文單字

ACROSS

3 難民
5 拉緊的、緊張的
6 煙霧、煙
10 小黃瓜
11 地平線、水平線
12 特權
14 改變
15 較好的

DOWN

1 反射、反省
2 恥辱的
4 糖漿
6 潛水艇
7 興盛、繁榮
8 踏板、踩踏板
9 普遍的、世界性的、宇宙的
13 歌劇

◆上面的遊戲會用到的單字都在這裡！真的看不懂提示就來偷瞄一下吧！

WORD BANK: Cucumber, horizon, opera, pedal, preferable, privilege, prosper, reflection, refugee, shameful, smog, submarine, syrup, tense, transform, universal.

答案就在後面

◆填字遊戲解答在這裡！

◆單字還記不熟嗎？快來做複習！

cucumber [ˈkjukʌmbɚ]	**refugee** [ˌrɛfjʊˈdʒi]
小黃瓜 a long thin round vegetable with a green skin and usually eaten raw	難民 someone who has been forced to leave their country in order to escape war or political, religious reasons
horizon [həˈraɪzn̩]	**shameful** [ˈʃemfəl]
地平線、水平線 the line where the sky seems to meet the earth	恥辱的 disgraceful, causing shame
opera [ˈɑpərə]	**smog** [smɑg]
歌劇 a musical play in which many or all of the words are sung	煙霧、煙 smoke and fog
pedal [ˈpɛdl̩]	**submarine** [ˈsʌbməˌrin]
踏板、踩踏板 a bar like part of a machine which can be pressed with the foot in order to control the working of the machine or to drive it	潛水艇 a ship especially a military one, that you can stay under the sea
preferable [ˈprɛfərəl]	**syrup** [ˈsɪrəp]
較好的 that one should or would prefer	糖漿 a thick sweet liquid made from sugar and water
privilege [ˈprɪvl̩ɪdʒ]	**tense** [tɛns]
特權 a special right or favor for a particular person or groups	拉緊的、緊張的 becoming tight and stiff
prosper [ˈprɑspɚ]	**transform** [trænsˈfɔrm]
興盛、繁榮 to become successful and rich	改變 to completely change the form or character of something to make them improve
reflection [rɪˈflɛkʃən]	**universal** [ˌjunəˈvɝsl̩]
反射、反省 the act of thinking over; the state of reflecting	普遍的、世界性的、宇宙的 involving everybody in the world

26

◆用中文解釋猜猜英文單字

ACROSS

1 提供資訊的、教育性的
3 支配、搖擺
6 推翻、瓦解
7 計算
12 搬運工
13 中間體、調解人、媒介物
14 主題、題目
15 結果、成果
16 有影響力的

DOWN

2 教師、指導者
4 發明、創造
5 分配、配給
8 落後
9 和……起衝突、反對
10 苦幹、努力
11 趕上、突擊

◆上面的遊戲會用到的單字都在這裡！真的看不懂提示就來偷瞄一下吧！

WORD BANK: Calculation, distribution, influential, informative, instructor, intermediate, invention, lag, oppose, outcome, overtake, overthrow, porter, strive, sway, theme.

答案就在後面

◆填字遊戲解答在這裡！

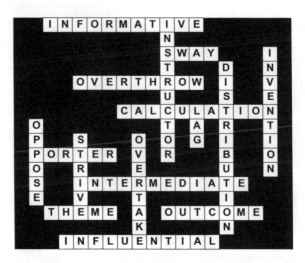

◆單字還記不熟嗎？快來做複習！

calculation [ˈkælkjəˌlet] 計算 to count mathematically	oppose [əˈpoz] 和……起衝突、反對 to have a fight against or to disagree with something
distribution [ˌdɪstrəˈbjuʃən] 分配、配給 the process of distributing	outcome [ˈaʊtˌkʌm] 結果、成果 the final result
influential [ˌɪnfluˈɛnʃəl] 有影響力的 powerful, effective	overtake [ˌovəˈtek] 趕上、突擊 to pass while going in order to get in front of them
informative [ɪnˈfɔrmətɪv] 提供資訊的、教育性的 giving many facts or ideas	overthrow [ˌovəˈθro] 推翻、瓦解 to remove a leader or government from power especially by force
instructor [ɪnˈstrʌktə] 教師、指導者 a person who is teaching something or whose job is to teach	porter [ˈportə] 搬運工 one who carries luggage; baggage man
intermediate [ˌɪntəˈmidɪɪt] 中間體、調解人、媒介物 something or someone in the middle	strive [straɪv] 苦幹、努力 to make great efforts to achieve something
invention [ɪnˈvɛnʃən] 發明、創造 the action of creating something	sway [swe] 支配、搖擺 to move slowly backwards and forwards
lag [læg] 落後 to move or develop more slowly	theme [θim] 主題、題目 the main subject or idea on speaking, writing, or thinking

27

◉ 捷徑文化版權所有

◆用中文解釋猜猜英文單字

ACROSS

1 預防
4 應景的、偶爾的
5 閃耀、點燃、鼓舞
8 壯觀的、華麗的
10 地位、身分
13 交互影響、互動
15 嚴厲的、嚴重的
16 實現、完成

DOWN

2 辭職、使順從
3 輕微的
6 娛樂、消遣
7 侵略、入侵
9 家庭、家用的、為人熟知的
11 閃爍、發光
12 單數
14 隱退、退休

◆上面的遊戲會用到的單字都在這裡！真的看不懂提示就來偷瞄一下吧！

WORD BANK: Fulfillment, household, interaction, invade, magnificent, occasional, prevention, recreation, resign, retire, severe, singular, slight, spark, status, twinkle.

答案就在後面

◆填字遊戲解答在這裡！

```
      P R E V E N T I O N
      E
      S           S
O C C A S I O N A L   S P A R K
      G           I             E
    I G   M A G N I F I C E N T
  H   N       H           R
  O   V   S T A T U S     E       S
  U   A   W               A       I
  S   D   I N T E R A C T I O N   N
S E V E R E   N       E       I   G
  E       N   K       T       O   U
  H       O   L       I           L
F U L F I L L M E N T         R   A
  D                           E   R
```

◆單字還記不熟嗎？快來做複習！

fulfillment [fu'fɪlmənt] 實現、完成 the feeling of being satisfied with your life	**resign** [rɪ'zaɪn] 辭職、使順從 to quit a job; to make yeilded
household ['haʊs,hold] 家庭、家用的、為人熟知的 a family	**retire** [rɪ'taɪr] 隱退、退休 to leave one's job and work no longer because of age
interaction [ˌɪntə'ækʃən] 交互影響、互動 a state when two or more things affect each other	**severe** [sə'vɪr] 嚴厲的、嚴重的 extreme serious and strict
invade [ɪn'ved] 侵略、入侵 to come into a place forcibly and attack	**singular** ['sɪŋgjələ] 單數 the form of a word used when talking about one person or thing
magnificent [mæg'nɪfəsənt] 壯觀的、華麗的 beautiful in a grand way which is impressive	**slight** [slaɪt] 輕微的 very little
occasional [ə'keʒənl] 應景的、偶爾的 not regular	**spark** [spɑrk] 閃耀、點燃、鼓舞 a small piece of burning material
prevention [prɪ'vɛnʃən] 預防 the act of preventing	**status** ['stetəs] 地位、身分 position, condition
recreation [ˌrɛkrɪ'eʃən] 娛樂、消遣 amusement, entertainment	**twinkle** ['twɪŋkl] 閃爍、發光 a small bright shining light that changes from bright to faint repeatedly

28

◆用中文解釋猜猜英文單字

ACROSS

1 繁榮的
7 值得紀念的
11 組織、建立
12 學問、學識
13 加強、增強
14 不情願的
15 職業
16 使閃耀

DOWN

2 保留
3 海鷗
4 雪橇
5 相對的、有關係的
6 可攜帶的
8 建築、結構
9 有毒的
10 有利的

◆上面的遊戲會用到的單字都在這裡！真的看不懂提示就來偷瞄一下吧！

WORD BANK: Construction, establishment, learning, memorable, occupation, poisonous, portable, profitable, prosperous, relative, reluctant, reservation, seagull, sleigh, sparkle, strengthen.

答案就在後面

Level-2

```
                      P R O S P E R O U S
                                  E                         R
              S           S       S               M E M O R A B L E
        P     E           L       R       P                       L
    C   O     A           E       V       O               P       A
    O   R     G           I       A       I               R       T
  E S T A B L I S H M E N T       T       S               O       I
    T   B     L           I       I       O               F       V
    R   L                 O       O       N               I       E
    U   E         L E A R N I N G         O               T
  S T R E N G T H E N     R E L U C T A N T
    I                             S               B
    O C C U P A T I O N                           L
    N               S P A R K L E
```

◆單字還記不熟嗎？快來做複習！

construction [kən'strʌkʃən]	prosperous ['prɑspərəs]
建築、結構 the process of building; a structure	繁榮的 rich and successful
establishment [ə'stæblɪʃ]	relative ['rɛlətɪv]
組織、建立 to start an organization or company that is intended to exist for a long time	相對的、有關係的 deemed as a comparation of something; connected or related
learning ['lɜnɪŋ]	reluctant [rɪ'lʌktənt]
學問、學識 knowledge or skill gained through studying	不情願的 unwilling
memorable ['mɛmərəbl]	reservation [ˌrɛzəˈveʃən]
值得紀念的 worth remembering	保留 feeling of doubt or uncertainty; the act of reserving
occupation [ˌɑkjəˈpeʃən]	seagull ['sigʌl]
職業 a job or profession	海鷗 a gray and white bird which lives near the sea
poisonous ['pɔɪznəs]	sleigh [sle]
有毒的 containing poison	雪橇 a sledge pulled by animals
portable ['portəbl]	sparkle [spɑrk]
可攜帶的 available for carrying or moving	使閃耀 to shimmer, glitter, glisten or to be brilliant
profitable ['prɑfɪtəbl]	strengthen ['strɛŋθən]
有利的 beneficial, yielding profit	加強、增強 to make something more powerful and stronger

29

◉ 捷徑文化版權所有

◆用中文解釋猜猜英文單字

ACROSS

2 機械
4 成熟期
5 運動員精神
8 監視器、螢幕
9 葡萄柚
12 發射
13 降雨量
15 可容忍的、可忍受的

DOWN

1 哲學家
3 發癢
6 重要性
7 誤導
10 明顯的
11 參考
12 執照、牌照
14 哭訴、啜泣

◆上面的遊戲會用到的單字都在這裡！真的看不懂提示就來偷瞄一下吧！

WORD BANK: Evident, grapefruit, itch, launch, license, machinery, maturity, mislead, monitor, philosopher, rainfall, reference, significance, sob, sportsmanship, tolerable.

答案就在後面

◆填字遊戲解答在這裡！

◆單字還記不熟嗎？快來做複習！

evident [ˈɛvədənt] 明顯的 obvious, easy to understand	**monitor** [ˈmɑnətɚ] 監視器、螢幕 a device that can record whatever happens in a certain place
grapefruit [ˈgrepˌfrut] 葡萄柚 a round yellow fruit with a thick skin and a sour juicy pulp, like a large orange	**philosopher** [fəˈlɑsəfɚ] 哲學家 a person who is an expert in philosophy
itch [ɪtʃ] 發癢 an uncomfortable feeling that makes you want to scratch the skin	**rainfall** [ˈrenˌfɔl] 降雨量 the amount of rain or snow that falls in an area in a certain time
launch [lɔntʃ] 發射 to start	**reference** [ˈrɛfərəns] 參考 an indication, as in a book or an article, of some other work or passage to be consulted
license [ˈlaɪsṇs] 執照、牌照 an official document allows someone to do something legally	**significance** [sɪgˈnɪfəkəns] 重要性 the importance
machinery [məˈʃinərɪ] 機械 machines	**sob** [sɑb] 哭訴、啜泣 to cry noisily while breathing in short, sudden bursts
maturity [məˈtjurətɪ] 成熟期 the time when someone or something is fully developed or grown	**sportsmanship** [ˈsportsmənʃɪp] 運動員精神 behavior that is fair, honest in a sports competition
mislead [mɪsˈlid] 誤導 to lead in a wrong direction	**tolerable** [ˈtɑlərəbl̩] 可容忍的、可忍受的 painful or unpleasant and just able to be accepted

30

◉ 捷徑文化版權所有

◆用中文解釋猜猜英文單字

ACROSS

1 集中、專心
3 手續
5 意向、意圖
9 佔有、花費（時間）
12 革命的
14 投資
15 被誤解的

DOWN

2 計畫、打算
3 現象
4 擊敗、克服
6 加強、增強
7 包容力、寬容
8 近視的
10 合夥
11 製造
13 調節、管理

◆上面的遊戲會用到的單字都在這裡！真的看不懂提示就來偷瞄一下吧！

WORD BANK: Concentration, intend, intensify, intention, invest, misunderstood, occupy, overcome, partnership, phenomenon, procedure, production, regulate, revolutionary, shortsighted, tolerance.

答案就在後面

◆填字遊戲解答在這裡！

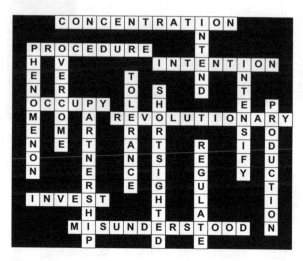

◆單字還記不熟嗎？快來做複習！

concentration [ˈkɑnsn̩ˌtret]	**partnership** [ˈpartnɚˌʃɪp]
集中、專心 to pay attention completely on something	合夥 the state of being a partner
intend [ɪnˈtɛnd]	**phenomenon** [fəˈnɑməˌnɑn]
計畫、打算 the thought to do something	現象 something that exists in society; circumstances
intensify [ɪnˈtɛnsəˌfaɪ]	**procedure** [prəˈsidʒɚ]
加強、增強 to become powerful	手續 a particular way of managing something
intention [ɪnˈtɛnʃən]	**production** [prəˈdʌkʃən]
意向、意圖 a determination to do a specific thing	製造 the act of producing something
invest [ɪnˈvɛst]	**regulate** [ˈrɛgjəˌlet]
投資 to put money to a particular use for the purpose of earning more money	調節、管理 to control by rules
misunderstood [ˌmɪsʌndɚˈstænd]	**revolutionary** [ˌrɛvəˈluʃənˌɛrɪ]
被誤解的 to fail to understand someone correctly	革命的 connected with or being a revolution
occupy [ˈɑkjəˌpaɪ]	**shortsighted** [ˈʃɔrtˈsaɪtɪd]
佔有、花費（時間） to take possession of by settlement or seizure	近視的 only able to see objects clearly when they are close
overcome [ˌovɚˈkʌm]	**tolerance** [ˈtɑlərəns]
擊敗、克服 to defeat; to conqure the weakness	包容力、寬容 the ability of enduring someone or something

THE END OF THIS LEVEL

用英文例句提示玩單字

Level-3

◉ 捷徑文化版權所有

◆用例句猜猜英文單字

ACROSS

3 His desire for money will lead him to his d___n one day; I wish he could understand that soon.
6 I don't suppose that cooking and washing are c___es.
7 I wish he could work hard enough to get his history d___a this year.
12 The course only deals with the e___ls of management, don't you make it out?
13 Would you please c___t on the conclusion?
14 It's windy and d___y here in spring; I wish I could move to another city next year.
15 Would you c___y her novels as literature or something else?
16 It was she who discovered the room in d___r first after work.

DOWN

1 Don't you see the bird on the balcony has a worm in its b___k?
2 It is no use in buying bags of this material; you'd better buy some canvas bags which are d___e instead.
4 P___y makes friends, adversity tries them, what do you think of it?
5 There wasn't enough e___e to prove his guilt.
8 He d___ted early in the morning so that he wouldn't miss the early train.
9 Why not be an a___c boy? Let's go to the gym together!
10 I'm too a___d to tell her that I had failed.
11 I am afraid that we have to look for another company because we find your price is not the most f___e.

◆上面的遊戲會用到的單字都在這裡！真的看不懂提示就來偷瞄一下吧！

WORD BANK: Ashamed, athletic, beak, chore, classify, comment, depart, destruction, diploma, disorder, durable, dusty, essential, evidence, favorable, prosperity.

083

答案就在後面

Level-3

◆填字遊戲解答在這裡！

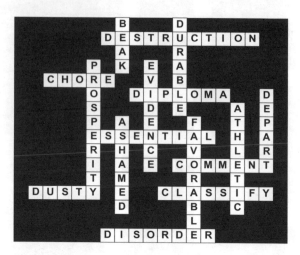

◆單字還記不熟嗎？快來做複習！

ashamed [əˋʃemd] 以……為恥、羞愧的 feeling guilty about something	**diploma** [dɪˋplomə] 文憑、畢業證書 a document showing that someone has completed a course of study
athletic [æθˋlɛtɪk] 運動的、強健的 physically strong, fit	**disorder** [dɪsˋɔrdɚ] 使混亂、混亂 uncontrolled, disorganized
beak [bik] 鳥嘴 a hard part of bird's mouth	**durable** [ˋdjurəbl̩] 耐穿的、耐磨的 staying in good condition for a long time
chore [tʃor] 雜事、打雜 a regular and required work, esp. in a house	**dusty** [ˋdʌstɪ] 覆著灰塵的 covered with dust
classify [ˋklæsəˏfaɪ] 分類 to decide what group something belongs to, to sort	**essential** [əˋsɛnʃəl] 本質的、必要的、基本的 something that is necessary
comment [ˋkɑmɛnt] 評語、評論 a note showing a judgment of an event	**evidence** [ˋɛvədəns] 證據 proof to tell what is true or valid
depart [dɪˋpɑrt] 離開、走開 to leave	**favorable** [ˋfevərəbl̩] 有利的、討人喜歡的 expressing approval
destruction [dɪˋstrʌkʃən] 破壞、損壞 the act of destroying something	**prosperity** [prɑsˋpɛrətɪ] 繁盛 good fortune and success

2

◉ 捷徑文化版權所有

◆用例句猜猜英文單字

ACROSS

2 Would you please c___e me another slice of meat?

3 Let us e___e all uncertainty on thought, will you?

4 The n___r bomb is powerful enough to damage all these villages.

5 I believe that the theater has a seating c___y of more than 800.

8 I don't think that weak law e___t is the main problem.

11 The problem may not a___e, but there's no harm in keeping our powder dry.

12 Will you indulge my c___y and tell me how much it cost?

13 Lack of confidence is the biggest b___r to find a good job, don't you think so?

DOWN

1 There is no point in b___ting yourself a genius in public.

2 The kids are all hungry. It is no wonder that the kids soon c___ed all the food on the table.

5 It's very foolish of the c___r to expose his troop to unnecessary risks.

6 A quiet c___e sleeps in thunder; what do you think of that?

7 He is a professional in this area. It is no wonder that his a___s of the problem shows great insight.

9 No one raised any o_____n against this proposal.

10 You should go with me unless your view is c___y to mine.

11 It is a pity that I have never been to the Triumphal A___h.

◆上面的遊戲會用到的單字都在這裡！真的看不懂提示就來偷瞄一下吧！

WORD BANK: Analysis, arch, arise, barrier, boast, capacity, carve, commander, conscience, consume, contrary, curiosity, eliminate, enforcement, nuclear, objection.

答案就在後面

◆填字遊戲解答在這裡！

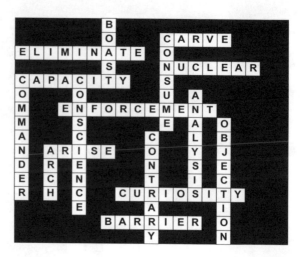

◆單字還記不熟嗎？快來做複習！

analysis [ə'næləsɪs] 分析 a separating or breaking up of any whole into its parts especially with a detailed examination	**conscience** ['kɑnʃəns] 良心 a person's moral sense of correct and incorrect
arch [ɑrtʃ] 拱門 something with a curved top and straight sides that supports the weight of a building	**consume** [kən'sum] 消耗、耗費 to eat or drink
arise [ə'raɪz] 出現、發生 to happen	**contrary** ['kɑntrɛrɪ] 矛盾 the opposite
barrier ['bærɪɚ] 障礙 anything that prevents movement or approach	**curiosity** [ˌkjʊrɪ'ɑsətɪ] 好奇心 the desire to know about something
boast [bost] 自誇 to talk proudly or show off abilities	**eliminate** [ɪ'lɪməˌnet] 消除 to remove; to get rid of
capacity [kə'pæsətɪ] 容積、能力 the amount that can be contained	**enforcement** [ɪn'forsmənt] 施行 to make people follow a rule or law
carve ['kɑrv] 雕刻 to cut into small pieces	**nuclear** ['njuklɪɚ] 核子的 relating to the nucleus of an atom
commander [kə'mændɚ] 指揮官 a person in high rank who is especially in charge of a particular military activity	**objection** [əb'dʒɛkʃən] 反對 a cause for opposing or disapproving of something you have

3

◉ 捷徑文化版權所有

◆用例句猜猜英文單字

ACROSS

4 It is their distinguishing c___c; what do you think of it?

6 It is no wonder that I can't access the file on your company because I've forgotten the c___e.

8 It is no wonder that in a b___k of an eye my brother has disappeared. He has a date with his grifriend today.

12 How about your h___n? Where did you go? Paris or London?

13 There is a small hole over there. It is no wonder that I can see a b___m of light in the cave.

14 Why not put on some m___p? It will make you more beautiful.

15 Would you like to tell me how to enquire about the i___n state?

16 Would you like to have some low fat y___t? It tastes very good.

DOWN

1 The foreign policy is not f___e enough to settle the international dispute.

2 Don't you think even a very small mistake would be f___l to our plan?

3 Jack ran away immediately as soon as the f___r was lit up.

5 Would you like to tell me how you are going to get through the a___t?

7 Bob hates biology. It is no wonder that he has been weak at b___y at school all these years.

9 Not everyone is willing to invest some time in c___y service.

10 It is a surprise that you should doubt his l___y to the company and the work.

11 I'm afraid that she can't a___t herself quickly to the new environment.

◆上面的遊戲會用到的單字都在這裡！真的看不懂提示就來偷瞄一下吧！

WORD BANK: Adapt, assignment, beam, biology, blink, characteristic, code, community, fatal, firecracker, flexible, honeymoon, immigration, loyalty, makeup, yogurt.

087

答案就在後面

◆填字遊戲解答在這裡！

◆單字還記不熟嗎？快來做複習！

adapt [ə`dæpt] 使適應 to gradually change something in order to become adjusted in a new situation	**fatal** [`fetl] 致命的、決定性的 resulting death; something important in its outcome
assignment [ə`saınmənt] 分派、任命 a piece of work that is given to someone	**firecracker** [`faır‚krækə] 鞭炮 a small firework that explodes loudly
beam [bim] 光線、照耀、微笑 to smile warmly	**flexible** [`flɛksəbl] 有彈性的、易曲的 something that can be bent easily
biology [baı`ɑlədʒı] 生物學 the scientific study of living things	**honeymoon** [`hʌnı‚mun] 蜜月 a holiday taken by a couple who have just got married
blink [blıŋk] 眨眼、閃爍 to close and open the eyes rapidly	**immigration** [‚ımə`greʃən] （從外地）移居入境 the process of living in another country
characteristic [‚kærıktə`rıstık] 特徵 traits of a particular thing or person	**loyalty** [`lɔıəltı] 忠誠 the state of being supportive
code [kod] 代號、編碼 a system of words, letters, or symbols used to be understood by someone who knows the system	**makeup** [`mekʌp] 結構、化妝 colored substances that are put on your face to change or improve your appearance
community [kə`mjunətı] 社區 a group of people who live in the same area	**yogurt** [`jogət] 優酪乳、優格 a thick liquid food that tastes slightly sour and is made from milk

4

◉ 捷徑文化版權所有

◆用例句猜猜英文單字

ACROSS

1 Her style was c___t with her personality; what do you think of that?

3 What a b___n! This beautiful dress just cost me fifty dollars

6 You are not mature enough; it is no wonder that I d___r with your opinion on this matter.

7 Let's have a f___l party before we leave, shall we?

10 Don't you think he is a d___e and hard-working worker?

12 The government must take actions at once, or we will have another Great D___n.

13 Not all people can stand firm a___d temptations.

14 Not everyone has a___s to the full facts of the case.

DOWN

1 It's disgraceful of him to make fun of a c___e.

2 It is no wonder that he successfully n___es a new contract with her company because he talks responsibly

4 Don't you know that adverbs are used to modify verbs and a___es?

5 There will be an international c___e held in London next month.

6 It is quite clear that genius is nothing but labor and d___e.

8 I appreciate her g___y in this matter; what do you think of that?

9 Beauty without virtue is a rose without f___e; what do you think of it?

11 She thought a problem for one night. It is obvious that that is a great a___y to her.

◆上面的遊戲會用到的單字都在這裡！真的看不懂提示就來偷瞄一下吧！

WORD BANK: Access, adverb, amid, anxiety, bargain, conference, consonant, cripple, dependable, depression, differ, diligence, farewell, fragrance, generosity, negotiate.

089

答案就在後面

◆填字遊戲解答在這裡！

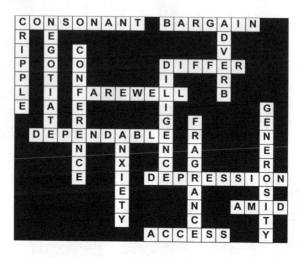

◆單字還記不熟嗎？快來做複習！

access [ˈæksɛs] 接近、使用或進入權、入口 way of approach, entry	**dependable** [dɪˈpɛndəbl] 可靠的 able to be trusted to do what you expect
adverb [ˈædvɚb] 副詞 word or phrase that alters the meaning of an adjective, verb, or other adverb	**depression** [dɪˈprɛʃən] 下陷、降低、沮喪、蕭條 the feeling of being dejected
amid [əˈmɪd] 在……之中 among or surrounded by things	**differ** [ˈdɪfɚ] 不同、相異 to be different from something
anxiety [æŋˈzaɪətɪ] 憂慮、不安、渴望 worry or concern about what may happen	**diligence** [ˈdɪlədʒəns] 勤勉、勤奮 care and take responsibilities in one's work
bargain [ˈbɑrgɪn] 協議、成交、討價還價 a mutual agreement made between parties as to determine what should be given or done by each	**farewell** [ˈfɛrˈwɛl] 告別、歡送會 a party or an event you have because you are leaving a city, or job
conference [ˈkɑnfərəns] 招待會、會議 a formal meeting where people discuss important matters	**fragrance** [ˈfregrəns] 芬香、芬芳 a pleasant smell
consonant [ˈkɑnsənənt] 子音、和諧的 a speech sound made by partly stopping the flow of air through the mouth	**generosity** [ˌdʒɛnəˈrɑsətɪ] 慷慨、寬宏大量 willingness to give or share
cripple [ˈkrɪpl̩] 瘸子、殘疾人 someone who is incapable to walk properly	**negotiate** [nɪˈgoʃɪet] 商議、談判 try to reach an agreement especially in business or politics

Level-3

5

◆用例句猜猜英文單字

ACROSS

1 It is no wonder that she heard nothing but the c____ps of insects.
3 It is obvious that they are unwilling to give us a d___e answer.
6 Life is compared to a v___e, and it takes everyone a lifetime to finish it.
8 I don't think that all people know that matters c___t of atoms.
12 Tom suggested to have a party on the weekend at his house; it is no wonder that the proposal was greeted with great e___m.
14 He felt shame at his bankruptcy . It is no wonder that he resolved never to tell anyone about this i___t.
15 Since you have a headache, why not take an a___n?

DOWN

1 Could you tell me how long it will take to discharge of the c___o?
2 This election d___ed democracy in action, what do you think about it?
4 Don't you think that she is e___s of Mary's slim figure?
5 As soon as it was published, the book had a big c___n.
7 M___e tests the sincerity of friends, don't you think so?
9 Why not use a simple example to i___e the point?
10 There is a war now. It is no wonder that the government wants c___ns to become soldiers.
11 I am afraid the population here will d___e year by year.
13 It is obvious that you a___h all the blame to the taxi-driver.

◆上面的遊戲會用到的單字都在這裡！真的看不懂提示就來偷瞄一下吧！

WORD BANK: Aspirin, attach, cargo, chirps, circulation, civilian, consist, decrease, definite, demonstrate, enthusiasm, envious, illustrate, incident, misfortune, voyage.

答案就在後面

◆填字遊戲解答在這裡！

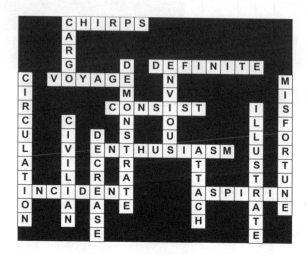

◆單字還記不熟嗎？快來做複習！

aspirin [ˈæspərɪn] 阿斯匹林 a medicine that reduces pain and fever	**definite** [ˈdɛfənɪt] 確定的 clear and precise
attach [əˈtætʃ] 連接、附屬、附加 to join	**demonstrate** [ˈdɛmənˌstret] 展現、表明 to prove something clearly
cargo [ˈkɑrgo] 貨物、船貨 goods which is carried by a large vehicle like a ship or truck	**enthusiasm** [ɪnˈθjuzɪˌæzəm] 熱衷、熱情 a strong feeling of interest and eagerness to be involved in it
chirp [tʃɜp] 蟲鳴鳥叫 to make the short sharp sound of small birds or insects	**envious** [ˈɛnvɪəs] 羨慕的、妒忌的 showing envy
circulation [ˌsɜkjəˈleʃən] 通貨、循環、發行量 movement through a circuit, especially the movement of blood through the body	**illustrate** [ˈɪləstret] 舉例說明 to make something clear by giving examples
civilian [səˈvɪljən] 平民、一般人 a common person	**incident** [ˈɪnsədənt] 事件 something that happens
consist [kənˈsɪst] 組成、構成 be composed of	**misfortune** [mɪsˈfɔrtʃən] 不幸 ill fortune, bad luck
decrease [ˈdɪkris] 減少、減小 to go down to a lower level	**voyage** [ˈvɔɪɪdʒ] 旅行、航海 a long trip in a ship or spacecraft

6

◉ 捷徑文化版權所有

◆用例句猜猜英文單字

ACROSS

3 Not all people can understand such abstract c___t easily.

4 Will you tell me when these plants b___m? In spring or summer?

6 Would you like to let me know if you have ever used an A___M to get money out?

9 Why not go back to your h___d since you miss it so much?

12 It won't be long before you find that he is d___d in many different spheres.

14 It is impossible for us to meet the d___e because of the terrible weather.

15 I suppose we shall be having some sort of c___n for the bride, don't you think so?

DOWN

1 There are many a___ies of our company in major cities of the country.

2 Family is largely influential to one's f_____n of character.

3 Please send me your current c___e as soon as possible.

5 This g___s living isn't for me; I prefer a simple life.

7 Not all surgeons really understand the g___m theory.

8 It is obvious that this essay is a___e in all respects.

10 We can't help asking ourselves that what to do after the earthquake d___r.

11 Once you promise someone, you must f___l it by all means.

13 Why not tie up the package well with heavy c___d?

◆上面的遊戲會用到的單字都在這裡！真的看不懂提示就來偷瞄一下吧！

WORD BANK: Admirable, agency, atm, bloom, catalogue, celebration, concept, cord, deadline, disaster, distinguished, formation, fulfill, germ, gracious, homeland.

093

答案就在後面

◆填字遊戲解答在這裡！

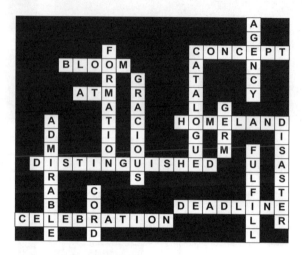

◆單字還記不熟嗎？快來做複習！

admirable [ˈædmərəb]] 令人欽佩的 having many good qualities that you respect	**deadline** [ˈdɛdˌlaɪn] 限期、截止日期 the latest time or date by which something should be done
agency [ˈedʒənsɪ] 代理商、代理機構 a business organization offering a particular kind of assistance	**disaster** [dɪzˈæstɚ] 天災、災害 an unexpected accident such as flood, earthquake which causes harm and suffering
ATM=Automatic Teller Machine [ˌɔtəˈmætɪk ˈtɛlɚ məˈʃin] 自動櫃員機 a machine outside a bank that you can get money from your account	**distinguished** [dɪˈstɪŋgwɪʃt] 卓越的 outstanding
bloom [blum] 開花期、開花 a period of time which plants grow flowers	**formation** [fɔrˈmeʃən] 形成、成立 the process of starting a new organization
catalogue [ˈkætəlɔg] 目錄 a list of things that you can look at	**fulfill** [fʊlˈfɪl] 實踐、實現、履行 to consummate something
celebration [ˌsɛləˈbreʃən] 慶祝、慶祝典禮 an occasion or party when you celebrate something	**germ** [dʒɝm] 細菌、微生物 a micro-organism esp. one of the bacteria
concept [ˈkɑnsɛpt] 概念 a thought or principle	**gracious** [ˈgreʃəs] 親切的、溫和有禮的、雅緻的 very polite and kind
cord [kɔrd] 電線 a thick long string	**homeland** [ˈhomˌlænd] 祖國、家鄉 the country where a person was born

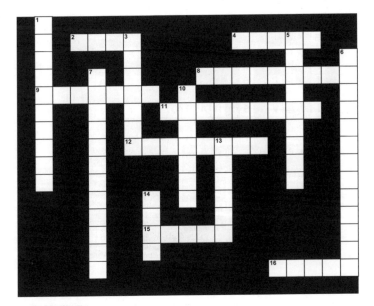

● 捷徑文化版權所有

◆用例句猜猜英文單字

ACROSS

2 Would you please get me an ice
c___e out of the fridge?
4 There is no point in going over the
d___t when it hasn't been finished
yet.
8 I don't think I can do it alone. Let's
c___e.
9 Not everyone knows that Canberra is
the c___l of Australia.
11 It is obvious that your mum suffered
too many h___ps in the past.
12 It is obvious that no one can remain
y___l forever.
15 It was too rainy to play outside, so
she a___ed herself with a book.
16 Why not buy a b___n of this kind?
It's more durable.

DOWN

1 They have a good general manager;
it is no wonder that their working
e___y is so high.
3 The e___y has been an obvious
target for terrorist attacks, don't you
think so?
5 We won't move the portrait hung
above the f___e unless we move into
a new house.
6 I don't think he has the d___n to
overcome this difficulty.
7 It has taken thousands of years for
mankind to realize the c___n.
10 Don't forget to charge the b___y at
night, or you can't call others
tomorrow.
13 Why not seize the chance and mount
a f___e attack?
14 The surface of the pond is full of
f___m; let's clear it up.

◆上面的遊戲會用到的單字都在這裡！真的看不懂提示就來偷瞄一下吧！

WORD BANK: Amuse, basin, battery, capital, civilization, cooperate, cube, determination, draft, efficiency, embassy, fierce, fireplace, foam, hardships, youthful.

095

答案就在後面

◆填字遊戲解答在這裡！

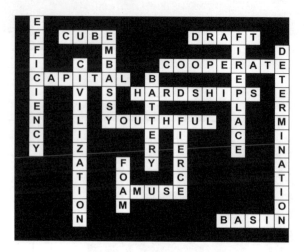

◆單字還記不熟嗎？快來做複習！

amuse [ə`mjuz] 娛樂、消遣 to make someone laugh	**draft** [dræft] 撰寫、草擬 a piece of writing or plan that is not yet finished
basin [`besn̩] 盆、水盆 a large bowl for food or liquids	**efficiency** [ə`fɪʃənsɪ] 效率 the state of doing something well
battery [`bætərɪ] 電池 a thing that provides a supply of electricity for something	**embassy** [`ɛmbəsɪ] 大使館 the officials who represent their government in a foreign country
capital [`kæpət̩l] 資本、首都、大寫字母 money or property used to start a new business or to produce more wealth	**fierce** [fɪrs] 猛烈的、粗暴的、兇猛的 very violent and savage
civilization [ˌsɪvl̩ə`zeʃən] 文明 human society that is well-organized and developed	**fireplace** [`faɪrˌples] 壁爐、火爐 a space in the wall of a room, where you can make a fire
cooperate [ko`ɑpəˌret] 合作 to work together towards the same direction	**foam** [fom] 泡沫 a mass of small bubbles on the surface of liquid
cube [kjub] 立方體、正六面體 a solid object with six equal square sides	**hardship** [`hɑrdʃɪp] 艱難、辛苦 difficult circumstances of life
determination [dɪˌtɜmə`neʃən] 決心 solution, firmness of purpose and mind	**youthful** [`juθfəl] 年輕的 young or characteristic of young people

8

◉ 捷徑文化版權所有

◆ 用例句猜猜英文單字

ACROSS

3 Would you please tell me how many c___t members the president has?

6 This play is awful. It is no wonder that it is d___ned by the reviewers.

9 You must intuit an i___m, or you cannot reason it out.

10 Didn't you see she turns away in d___t? What on earth did you say?

12 I had a quick d___e on the train, or I couldn't continue working after the journey.

14 I've had enough of her c___l talk; what about you?

15 He likes to help people a lot; it is no wonder that he decides to d___e himself to becoming a doctor.

16 Tom studied very hard; it is no wonder that he can speak f___t English.

DOWN

1 I think your new secretary is too c___g to believe.

2 Will you tell me why she f___ds me to call her late at night?

4 Common interests formed a b___d between us.

5 He felt a great deal of pain in his a___n.

7 I don't think that most of the young people nowadays have respect for a___y.

8 It's too hard for me to c___e him of the reality of the danger.

11 Can you tell me how long you have studied b___t up to now?

13 It is his good name that brings him e___s success.

◆ 上面的遊戲會用到的單字都在這裡！真的看不懂提示就來偷瞄一下吧！

WORD BANK: Abdomen, authority, ballet, bond, cabinet, continual, convince, cunning, damn, devote, disgust, doze, enormous, fluent, forbid, idiom.

答案就在後面

Level-3

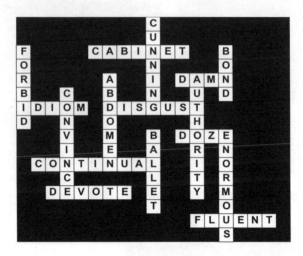

◆單字還記不熟嗎？快來做複習！

abdomen [ˋæbdəmən] 腹部 stomach, belly	**damn** [dæm] 指責、輕蔑 to blame someone or something strongly
authority [əˋθɔrətɪ] 權威、當局 the power or right to give commands or take action	**devote** [dɪˋvot] 貢獻、奉獻 to spend most of your time doing or helping people
ballet [ˋbæle] 芭蕾 an artistic dance form based on an elaborate formal technique	**disgust** [dɪsˋgʌst] 厭惡 a strong feeling of dislike
bond [bɑnd] 契約、束縛、聯結 a written agreement to do something	**doze** [doz] 打瞌睡 a short sleep
cabinet [ˋkæbənɪt] 小櫥櫃、內閣 a storage section for clothes and costly possession	**enormous** [ɪˋnɔrməs] 巨大的 very big in size
continual [kənˋtɪnjʊəl] 連續的 happening without stopping	**fluent** [ˋfluənt] 流暢的、流利的 speaking or writing smoothly
convince [kənˋvɪns] 說服、信服 to persuade someone to believe completely about something	**forbid** [fɚˋbɪd] 禁止 that something is not allowed
cunning [ˋkʌnɪŋ] 精明的、狡猾的 someone who is clever and good at planning something just to get what they want	**idiom** [ˋɪdɪəm] 成語、慣用語 a group of words that has a special meaning that is different from the usual mean ing of each individual word

9

◉ 捷徑文化版權所有

◆用例句猜猜英文單字

ACROSS

4 Do you know if there is intelligent life e___e in the universe?

5 This week there's a painting e___t at the art gallery, why not go see it with us?

6 Don't you believe a d___e man will stop at nothing to get what he wants?

9 It is hard for our country to keep p___e with other developed country.

13 I don't think he sent the present in e___t.

14 I don't believe she will willingly put up with his c___y to her.

15 I am afraid that we can't b___l turkey over the fire tonight.

16 This house is an old building. It is no wonder that there are so many c___ks in the wall.

DOWN

1 Do you mind if I b___d a dog in our house? I really like dogs very much.

2 I don't think they are very much interested in your h___e.

3 There is no good in adopting d___e attitudes; our plan is doomed to failure.

7 The company made much money last year. It is no wonder that the company made an a___t in my salary.

8 China is striding ahead in her e___c construction, don't you think so?

10 Not all citizens have the rights of a___y and expression in that country.

11 Not all the people are brave enough to face the b___l reality in their life.

12 What do you think about the idea that I apply for a job as a mail c___r?

◆上面的遊戲會用到的單字都在這裡！真的看不懂提示就來偷瞄一下吧！

WORD BANK: Adjustment, assembly, breed, broil, brutal, carrier, crack, cruelty, defensive, desperate, earnest, economic, elsewhere, exhibit, hardware, pace.

答案就在後面

Level-3

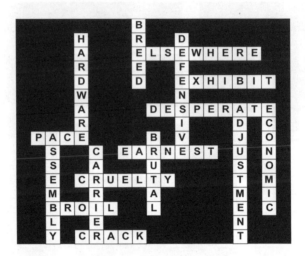

◆單字還記不熟嗎？快來做複習！

adjustment [ə`dʒʌstmənt] 調整、調節 a small change	defensive [dɪ`fɛnsɪv] 防禦的、保衛的 intended to protect
assembly [ə`sɛmblɪ] 集會、集合、會議 a group of people gathered together for a general purpose	desperate [`dɛspərɪt] 絕望的 feeling hopeless
breed [brid] 生育、繁殖、品種 to give a birth to or generate descendant	earnest [`ɝnɪst] 認真的、誠摯的 very serious and sincere
broil [brɔɪl] 烤、炙 to cook meat or fish with intense heat	economic [ˌikə`namɪk] 經濟上的 relating to the economy
brutal [`brutl̩] 野蠻的、殘暴的 very mean and ruthlessly violent	elsewhere [`ɛlsˌhwɛr] 在別處 at other places
carrier [`kærɪɚ] 運送者、送信人 someone who carries something	exhibit [ɪg`zɪbɪt] 展示品、展覽 a collection of objects displayed in a museum or an art gallery
crack [kræk] 使爆裂、使破裂 a narrow opening between two parts of something which either has split or been broken	hardware [`hɑrdˌwɛr] 五金用品、設備 metal tools for your home or garden; equipment
cruelty [`kruəltɪ] 冷酷、殘忍 cruel behavior or manner that cause pain to people or animals	pace [pes] 一步、步調 rate or speed in walking, running, advance of a plan

10

◉ 捷徑文化版權所有

◆用例句猜猜英文單字

ACROSS

4 I don't think it's proper for you to give him a c___r as a present.

6 It is obvious that the play c___xed in the third act.

8 He cares very little for f___e and fortune.

13 My dream is to be a c___r when I was young; what about you?

14 Because people don't want to be delayed, it is no wonder that the plane took off d___e the fog.

15 It is no wonder that the novel should be read in c___n with the author's biography.

16 From the Internet, you can d___d not only e-books but also movies.

DOWN

1 There are many people regularly giving money to c___y.

2 I don't like the d___p weather in this city; what about you?

3 It doesn't matter if my clothes are made of c___e cloth.

5 I think imagination is the source of c___n; what do you think of that?

7 How to gain the a___n to the Buckingham Palace? That's really a question!

9 Would you like to tell me what the best a___n in New York is?

10 It was the teacher's a___n that made me study much harder.

11 Nothing can a___e permanent happiness, don't you think so?

12 Does the wisteria b___m this year? Let's go to the park and have a look.

◆上面的遊戲會用到的單字都在這裡！真的看不懂提示就來偷瞄一下吧！

WORD BANK: Admiration, admission, assure, attraction, blossom, calculator, charity, climax, coarse, conductor, conjunction, creation, damp, despite, download, fame.

答案就在後面

Level-3

◆填字遊戲解答在這裡！

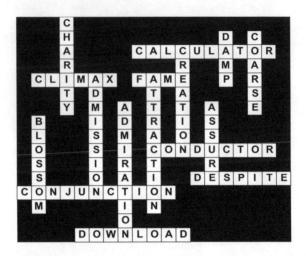

◆單字還記不熟嗎？快來做複習！

admiration [ˌædməˈreʃən] 欽佩、讚賞 a feeling of great respect	**coarse** [kors] 粗糙的、粗俗的 rough
admission [ədˈmɪʃən] 准許進入、入場費 entrance fee	**conductor** [kənˈdʌktə] 指揮、指導者 someone who directs an orchestra
assure [əˈʃʊr] 向……保證、使確信 to tell someone that something is definitely true so that they are less worried	**conjunction** [kənˈdʒʌŋkʃən] 連接、關聯 a combination of different things
attraction [əˈtrækʃən] 魅力、吸引力 charming	**creation** [krɪˈeʃən] 創造、創世 the process of creating
blossom [ˈblɑsəm] 花、生長茂盛 to produce flowers	**damp** [dæmp] 潮濕的 slightly wet
calculator [ˈkælkjəˌletə] 計算機 an electronic device for making mathematical operations	**despite** [dɪˈspaɪt] 不管、不顧 in spite of
charity [ˈtʃærətɪ] 慈悲、慈善、寬容 kindness and sympathy	**download** [ˈdaʊnˌlod] 下載 to move data from one computer system to another
climax [ˈklaɪmæks] 頂點、高潮 the most exciting and important part in a story	**fame** [fem] 名聲、聲譽 the state of being known by many people because you have achieved something

11

◉ 捷徑文化版權所有

◆用例句猜猜英文單字

ACROSS

4 Could you tell me what do you think of the a___e?

6 Not all people by the sea notice a tiny fishing boat d___ting slowly along.

7 The actor missed his c___e and came onto the stage late.

8 Let's c___e ourselves on our narrow escape.

14 Not all people know the c___n of the United Nations Organization.

15 You must keep away from l___r and tobacco, or your illness will get worse.

16 By the time my father was about to leave the house, he asked me to f___h his coat.

DOWN

1 The hotel lobby has a display of local c___ts; let's go and have a look.

2 The g___s are now in transit; why not wait for a few more days?

3 Will you tell me why they built the castle in the d___t position above the town?

5 It was c___s of him to oppose his boss.

9 It is quite clear that a light of g___e came into her eyes.

10 Why not put on your e___e and try the equipment?

11 I am afraid it's time for me to write an a___l report.

12 So many good ideas! It's too much for me to a___b all at once.

13 I wish scientists could find more dinosaur f___ls so that we could know more about dinosaurs.

◆上面的遊戲會用到的單字都在這裡！真的看不懂提示就來偷瞄一下吧！

WORD BANK: Absorb, annual, article, congratulate, constitution, courageous, craft, cue, dominant, drift, earphone, fetch, fossil, goods, gratitude, liquor.

答案就在後面

◆填字遊戲解答在這裡！

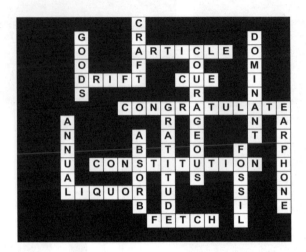

◆單字還記不熟嗎？快來做複習！

absorb [əb`sɔrb] 吸收 to suck up a liquid or another material	**dominant** [`dɑmənənt] 支配的 ruling, controlling
annual [`ænjʊəl] 一年的、年度的 happening once a year	**drift** [drɪft] 漂移 to move slowly on water
article [`ɑrtɪkl̩] 文章、論文 a piece of writing	**earphone** [`ɪr͵fon] 耳機 an electrical equipment worn on the ear to listen to music or radio
congratulate [kən`grætʃə͵let] 恭喜 to show happiness or praise to someone because they have achieved something	**fetch** [fɛtʃ] 取得、接來、去拿來 bring something back
constitution [͵kɑnstə`tjuʃən] 憲法、構造 the system of laws and principles, usually written down, according to which a country or an organization is regulated	**fossil** [`fɑsl̩] 化石、陳舊的 the remains of a plant or animal embedded in rock and preserved for a long time
courageous [kə`redʒəs] 勇敢的 brave, valiant	**goods** [gʊdz] 商品 merchandise
craft [kræft] 手工藝 a job or an activity involving skill in making things by hand	**gratitude** [`grætə͵tjud] 感激、感謝 feeling thankful; appreciating
cue [kju] 暗示 a hint, an action that is a signal for something else to happen	**liquor** [`lɪkɚ] 烈酒 a strong alcoholic drink

12

◉ 捷徑文化版權所有

◆用例句猜猜英文單字

ACROSS

1 I don't think this famous team d___ded well enough in the game.
4 There are many household a___es in this shop.
7 It is obvious that his e___t clothes contrasted with his rough speech.
8 He is such a wonderful man. It is no wonder that she formed a strong a___t for him so soon.
12 The c___r economy is an effective way for sustainable development.
13 His c___y attempt to tell a joke made us laugh.
14 Each attack is also a d___e, what do you think about that?
15 It is hard for the young man to understand the old man who once met so many f___ns in his life.
16 Turmeric can also be used as a d___e; would you give me some?

DOWN

2 It is quite obvious that he is f___ring you; I guess he wants you to help him.
3 It is obvious that the b___y of Abraham Lincoln is popular in America.
5 I'm afraid that you will think I'm c___e. Won't you think so?
6 Why not give him any i___n of your feelings?
9 There is a misunderstanding between the company and me. It is no wonder that the goods don't c___d with my order.
10 This c___y is said to attribute to Shakespeare; what do you think of that?
11 I got surprised at the e___t of his knowledge.

◆上面的遊戲會用到的單字都在這裡！真的看不懂提示就來偷瞄一下吧！

WORD BANK: Appliance, attachment, biography, circular, clumsy, comedy, conservative, correspond, defend, defense, dye, elegant, extent, flatter, frustration, indication.

105

◆填字遊戲解答在這裡！

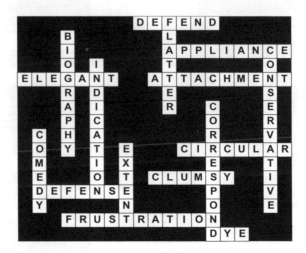

◆單字還記不熟嗎？快來做複習！

appliance [ə`plaɪəns] 器具、家電用品 a device or machine for performing a particular task	**defend** [dɪ`fɛnd] 保衛、防禦 to protect from danger
attachment [ə`tætʃmənt] 連接、附著 a part or condition attached to something	**defense** [dɪ`fɛns] 防禦 guarding against offense, harm or danger
biography [baɪ`ɑgrəfɪ] 傳記 the histories of individual lives	**dye** [daɪ] 染、著色 to change the colors of something
circular [`sɝkjələ] 圓形的、循環的、迂迴的 like a circle shape	**elegant** [`ɛləgənt] 優雅的 graceful and stylish
clumsy [`klʌmzɪ] 笨拙的 ungraceful in movement or presentation	**extent** [ɪk`stɛnt] 範圍、程度 area
comedy [`kɑmədɪ] 喜劇 a play, film, or TV program that is intended to make people laugh	**flatter** [`flætə] 諂媚、奉承 to give praise even though you don't actually mean it
conservative [kən`sɝvətɪv] 保守的、保守黨的、守舊的 someone who is not liking changes	**frustration** [ˌfrʌs`treʃən] 挫折、失敗 the feeling of being upset because you can not change a situation or achieve something
correspond [ˌkɔrə`spɑnd] 符合、相當 to harmonize with something almost exactly	**indication** [ˌɪndə`keʃən] 指示、表示 a sign that shows what is happening

13

◉ 捷徑文化版權所有

◆用例句猜猜英文單字

ACROSS

2 The prison is very small. It is no wonder that the prisoners were kept in a narrow c___r.

4 Health and good sense are the two b___gs of life; what do you think of it?

7 I wish you could i___e your elder brother a little more.

11 Why not try it in every conceivable c___n?

12 Spring makes everyone feel i___e.

13 There are quite a few people interested in seeing movies about American police and g___rs.

14 I found that it's very hard for me to c___y my feelings in words.

15 Could you tell me how to maximize the benefits of electronic c___e?

DOWN

1 This view is too new. It is no wonder that the view has not received wide a___e.

3 Let's a___t a day to have dinner together, OK?

4 It was the b___t that my husband bought to me as a gift for our wedding anniversary.

5 You will be put at a d___e unless you change your plan immediately.

6 I don't think the c___n matches the sofa. What do you think of that?

8 A slight error in thought may c___e a life-long regret, don't you think so?

9 It is the economic recession that caused the d___c market disappeared.

10 Not only professionals, but also a___rs can take part in the tournament.

◆上面的遊戲會用到的單字都在這裡！真的看不懂提示就來偷瞄一下吧！

WORD BANK: Acceptance, amateur, appoint, blessing, bracelet, chamber, combination, commerce, constitute, convey, cushion, disadvantage, dynamic, gangster, idle, imitate.

答案就在後面

◆填字遊戲解答在這裡！

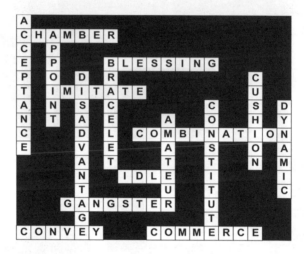

◆單字還記不熟嗎？快來做複習！

acceptance [ək`sɛptəns] 接受 agreement that something is proper could be accepted	**constitute** [`kɑnstə,tjut] 構成、制定 to be considered as something
amateur [`æmə,tʃur] 業餘的 someone who engages in an activity for the pleasure of it	**convey** [kən`ve] 傳達、運送 to transport or bring something to somewhere
appoint [ə`pɔɪnt] 任命、約定、指派、任用 to give someone a job or role	**cushion** [`kuʃən] 墊子、緩和……衝擊 a cloth bag filled with a mass of soft material that you put on a chair to make it more comfortable
blessing [`blɛsɪŋ] 恩典、祝福 the gift of divine favor	**disadvantage** [,dɪsəd`væntɪdʒ] 缺點、不利 something that causes problems
bracelet [`breslɪt] 手鐲 a band or chain worn on the wrist as a decoration	**dynamic** [daɪ`næmɪk] 動力的、有活力的 energetic, forceful
chamber [`tʃembɚ] 房間、寢室 a room	**gangster** [`gæŋstɚ] 歹徒、匪徒 a member of a violent group of criminals
combination [,kɑmbə`neʃən] 結合 the action of putting two or more things together	**idle** [`aɪdl̩] 閒置的 no working, having no value
commerce [`kɑmɝs] 商業、貿易 the activity of buying and selling goods and services	**imitate** [`ɪmə,tet] 仿效、效法 take as one's pattern, follow the example

14

◉ 捷徑文化版權所有

◆用例句猜猜英文單字

ACROSS

3 It was generous of her to c___e such a large sum.

6 They practiced very hard; it is no wonder that the team won a g___s victory again.

7 I don't know how to c___e with the problem of poor vision.

9 Would you like to do a quick e___n for me?

12 I don't think that he is the best c___e for the job.

13 I am afraid that I have to resign my child to the care of the n___y.

14 There are n___s stars shining in the sky; how beautiful they are!

15 I don't believe that it is the color resulting from the b___d.

16 From color a___t, we prefer this car; what about you?

DOWN

1 Let's find out what sort of f___l these new machines need.

2 Will you tell me how you laid the f___n of your success?

4 He broke the vase. It is no wonder that his mother was so a___yed with him.

5 Would you tell me what a___n you have with the color green?

8 Would you please send me an e___n? There is something wrong with my electric meter.

10 Would you like to offer us a life-time g___e?

11 It is said that there were hardly any dry eyes at the f___l.

◆上面的遊戲會用到的單字都在這裡！真的看不懂提示就來偷瞄一下吧！

WORD BANK: Annoy, aspect, association, blend, candidate, contribute, cope, electrician, evaluation, foundation, fuel, funeral, glorious, guarantee, numerous, nursery.

答案就在後面

Level-3

◆填字遊戲解答在這裡！

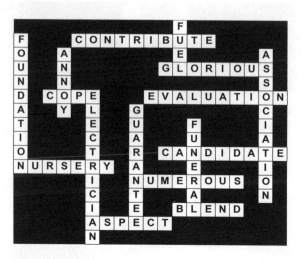

◆單字還記不熟嗎？快來做複習！

annoy [ə`nɔɪ] 煩擾、使惱怒 to irritate, bother or make slightly angry	**evaluation** [ɪˌvæljʊ`eʃən] 評價、估價 a judgment about how good or important something is
aspect [`æspɛkt] 方面、外貌、外觀 the appearance of a thing as seen from a particular viewpoint	**foundation** [faʊn`deʃən] 基礎、根基 the lowest base of a building or a structure
association [əˌsosɪ`eʃən] 協會、聯合會 a group of people organized for a special intention	**fuel** [`fjʊə] 燃料補給、燃料 material like wood, gas, or oil that is used for producing heat or power
blend [blɛnd] 混合、使交融 to mix thoroughly	**funeral** [`fjunərəl] 葬禮、告別式 a ceremony for burying or burning someone who has died
candidate [`kændəˌdet] 候選人 a person who is selected for an election	**glorious** [`glorɪəs] 著名的、榮耀的 deserving great fame, very famous
contribute [kən`trɪbjʊt] 貢獻 to give money, assistance...etc. in order to help achieve something	**guarantee** [ˌgærən`ti] 保證、保證人 a formal declaration that something will be done especially that a product will be of a good quality
cope [kop] 處理、對付 to deal with something	**numerous** [`njumərəs] 為數眾多的 many
electrician [ɪˌlɛk`trɪʃən] 電機工程師 someone who works related to electrical equipment	**nursery** [`nɝsərɪ] 托兒所 a place where young children are taken special care of

15

◉ 捷徑文化版權所有

◆用例句猜猜英文單字

ACROSS

2 He looked at her with a f___n, and found it was hard for him to talk about this matter.

4 Why not open a window to allow the air to c___e?

5 I hope that what I say will c___y the situation.

8 It is a pity that she a___ned her dream at last.

12 Will you tell me when you can finish the d___n of the living room?

13 She was c___t with the result.

14 Her mother is sick; it is no wonder that she had a major e___l upset.

15 What do you think of sending my mother an e___t of our baby's photo?

DOWN

1 You can avoid c_____n by speaking clearly.

3 It is obvious that the poor woman was buried in g___f after her son's death.

5 It is no wonder that the last five years have seen a c___t improvement in the country's economy.

6 Too much g___y food isn't good for your health.

7 I wish the speaker could c___e himself to the subject.

9 Will you tell me what is on the school b___n board today?

10 The black furnishings provide an interesting c___t to the white walls, don't you think so?

11 That scientist is very g___d. It is no wonder that he was much in the public eye.

◆上面的遊戲會用到的單字都在這裡！真的看不懂提示就來偷瞄一下吧！

WORD BANK: Abandon, bulletin, circulate, clarify, confine, confusion, consistent, content, contrast, decoration, emotional, enlargement, frown, gifted, greasy, grief.

答案就在後面

◆填字遊戲解答在這裡！

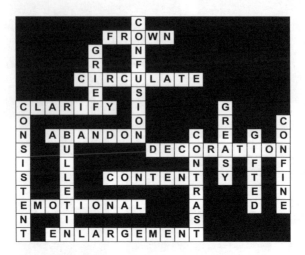

◆單字還記不熟嗎？快來做複習！

abandon [əˈbændən] 放棄、拋棄 to quit something before you have finished it	**consistent** [kənˈsɪstənt] 一致的、調和的 behaving in the same way always
bulletin [ˈbʊlətɪn] 公告、告示 a board or wall area on which displays are put up	**contrast** [ˈkɑnˌtræst] 對照 to compare in order to show difference
circulate [ˈsɝkjəˌlet] 循環 to move around within a system	**decoration** [ˌdɛkəˈreʃən] 裝飾 the process of decorating
clarify [ˈklærəˌfaɪ] 澄清、變得明晰 to make something more understandable	**emotional** [ɪˈmoʃənl̩] 情感的 quick to weep, be angry
confusion [kənˈfjuʒən] 迷惑、混亂 something that you don't understand because it is not clear	**enlargement** [ɪnˈlɑrdʒmənt] 擴張、（書）增訂、放大的照片 an increase in size
content [kənˈtɛnt] 內容、滿足、目錄 something that is contained	**gifted** [ˈgɪftɪd] 有天賦的、有才能的 having a natural ability in a particular region, talented
frown [fraʊn] 皺眉、表示不滿 to move your eyebrows together to show that you are worried or angry	**greasy** [ˈgrizɪ] 塗有油脂的、油膩的 covered with fat or oil
confine [kənˈfaɪn] 限制、侷限 to keep within limits; restrict	**grief** [grif] 悲傷、感傷 a feeling of sorrow

16

◉ 捷徑文化版權所有

◆用例句猜猜英文單字

ACROSS

2 She is an artist. It is no wonder that the interior design of her room is very a___c.

4 The longer you live here with your family, the more familiar you will get with the d___t.

6 I don't think that the temporary c___e of war means permanent peace.

9 In my opinion, only a truly free person has human d___y; what do you think of that?

11 It is necessary for soldiers to e___e discipline in the army.

13 It is quite clear that he didn't want to d___b his father at night.

14 My schedule is quite e___c.

15 It doesn't sound remarkable unless you examine it in c___t.

DOWN

1 It is obvious that she is Irish, because she speaks with an Irish a___t.

2 There is an a___e of peace and calm in the country, which is totally different from the city.

3 How to e___h a good credit policy? That's a problem.

5 There are a lot of spelling mistakes in your c___n.

7 A good salesman must be a___e if he wants to succeed; what do you think of that?

8 Honors do not always go to those who d___e them; what do you think about that?

10 Would you please insert a comment in the m___n?

12 Justice has long a___s, but not everyone knows this.

◆上面的遊戲會用到的單字都在這裡！真的看不懂提示就來偷瞄一下吧！

WORD BANK: Accent, aggressive, arms, artistic, atmosphere, cease, composition, context, deserve, dignity, district, disturb, elastic, enforce, establish, margin.

113

答案就在後面

◆填字遊戲解答在這裡！

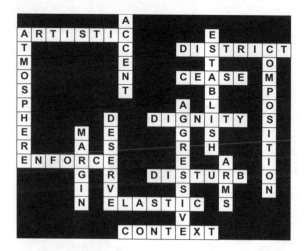

◆單字還記不熟嗎？快來做複習！

accent [`æksɛnt] 口音、腔調 the way how people pronounce the words of a language, showing which country or district	deserve [dɪ`zɜv] 值得、應得 to have earned something by good or bad actions
aggressive [ə`grɛsɪv] 侵略的、攻擊的 having or showing determination and energetic pursuit of your ends	dignity [`dɪgnətɪ] 威嚴、尊嚴 serious behavior that makes people respect you
arms [ɑrmz] 武器、兵器 weapons used for fighting wars	district [`dɪstrɪkt] 區域 an area of a region
artistic [ɑr`tɪstɪk] 藝術的、美術的 relating to art or artists	disturb [dɪ`stɜb] 使騷動、使不安 to interrupt, annoy
atmosphere [`ætməsˌfɪr] 大氣、氣氛 a particular environment or surrounding influence	elastic [ɪ`læstɪk] 有彈性的、靈活的 able to spring back to its original size, shape after being stretched, flexible
cease [sis] 終止、停止 to stop	enforce [ɪn`fors] 實施、強迫 to make people obey a rule or law
composition [ˌkɑmpə`zɪʃən] 組合、作文、混合物 the structure of something made up from different parts	establish [ə`stæblɪʃ] 建立 to start a company that is intended to exist for a long time
context [`kɑntɛkst] 上下文、文章脈絡 the parts of a piece of writing which influence to clarify its meaning	margin [`mɑrdʒɪn] 邊緣 an edge or brink

17

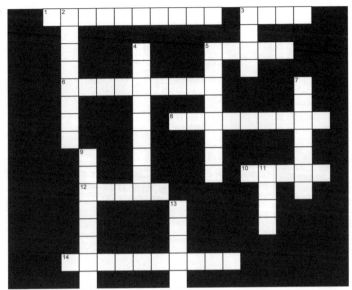

◉ 捷徑文化版權所有

◆用例句猜猜英文單字

ACROSS

1 I don't think that getting gold medals is the only dream of every c____r.

3 The c____k flew off with a pop; would you get it back for me?

5 Can't you see the b____e of the knife flash in the moonlight?

6 This painting is an i_____n of the one in the museum.

8 I guess there will be nothing left after the h____e, do you think so?

10 It is too difficult for them to accept those h____h facts you just said.

12 The father c_____ed angrily at his child.

14 Let us see all the official documents c____g the sale of this land.

DOWN

2 It is quite obvious that every citizen shall be o____t to the law.

3 I'm afraid that I need more time to c____m for the test.

4 There are ten of the e____s failing in the examination.

5 There was no man wanting to work in that factory. It is no wonder that the factory in the village went b____t last month.

7 There will be a composition c____t in July; would you like to join the contest?

9 The a____r of every action is a thought; what do you think of that?

11 We own more than 100 a____es of farmland; what about you?

13 I don't believe that his f____k in this final examination is true.

◆上面的遊戲會用到的單字都在這裡！真的看不懂提示就來偷瞄一下吧！

WORD BANK: Acre, ancestor, bankrupt, blade, competitor, concerning, contest, cork, cram, curse, examinees, flunk, harsh, hurricane, imitation, obedient.

115

Level-3

◆填字遊戲解答在這裡！

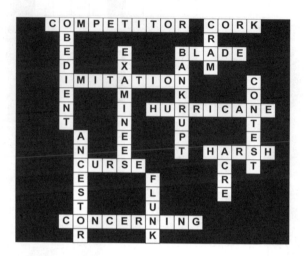

◆單字還記不熟嗎？快來做複習！

acre [ˋekɚ] 英畝、土地 a unit of area	**cram** [kræm] 把……塞進、狼吞虎嚥地吃東西 to compel something into something
ancestor [ˋænsɛstɚ] 祖先、祖宗 someone from whom you are descended but usually more distant than a grandparent	**curse** [kɝs] 詛咒、罵 to swear
bankrupt [ˋbæŋkrʌpt] 破產 a person who has insufficient property to cover their debts	**examinees** [ɪɡˏzæməˋni] 應試者 a person being or to be examined
blade [bled] 刀鋒 the cutting part of a tool or weapon	**flunk** [flʌŋk] 失敗、不及格 to fail a test
competitor [kəmˋpɛtətɚ] 競爭者 someone who takes part in a contest or competition	**harsh** [harʃ] 粗魯、令人不快的 cruel, unkind
concerning [kənˋsɝnɪŋ] 關於 about	**hurricane** [ˋhɝɪˏken] 颶風 a violent storm with a strong wind usually in the West Indian region
contest [ˋkɑntɛst] 與……競爭、爭奪 a competition in which people or groups are competing with each other	**imitation** [ˏɪməˋteʃən] 模仿、仿造品 when you copy the way someone behaves or speaks
cork [kɔrk] 軟木塞 a light brown material which is put into the top of a bottle to keep liquid inside	**obedient** [əˋbidɪənt] 服從的 doing what one is ordered to do

116

18

◉ 捷徑文化版權所有

◆用例句猜猜英文單字

ACROSS

2 Don't you think accidents have been happening with increasing f___y these years?

5 I hope you enjoyed your stay at the g___y.

8 What do you think of the d___l camera? It's the latest model this year.

11 I don't think he knows the exact d___e time of the flight.

13 Would you like to be her intimate friend and good c___n?

14 It is a surprise that no one should recognize her when she was in the d___e of a maid.

15 I don't think the enemy can occupy this f___t within a week.

16 It is easy for her to forget her basket in her h___e to leave.

DOWN

1 I wish our manager could agree to this plan without any h___n.

3 I don't think this will d___e him from continuing to have a try.

4 He doesn't want to make any commitment to anything he can't handle. It is no wonder that he would not c___t himself in any way.

6 It often takes us quite a long time to d___t new ideas.

7 No one is able to f___t how long the war will last.

9 I hope the arrangements will meet with your a___l.

10 No one knows that why this d___y disappeared suddenly a thousand years ago.

12 They are deeply in love with each other; it is no wonder that they can e___e long distance.

◆上面的遊戲會用到的單字都在這裡！真的看不懂提示就來偷瞄一下吧！

WORD BANK: Approval, commit, companion, departure, digest, digital, discourage, disguise, dynasty, endure, forecast, fort, frequency, gallery, haste, hesitation.

答案就在後面

◆填字遊戲解答在這裡！

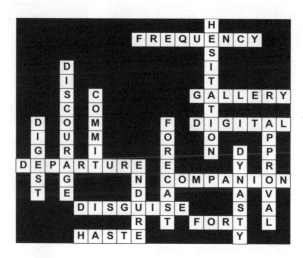

◆單字還記不熟嗎？快來做複習！

approval [ə`pruvl] 承認、同意 to admit or agree	**dynasty** [`daɪnəstɪ] 王朝、朝代 a period when a particular family ruled a country
commit [kə`mɪt] 委任、承諾、犯罪、做（錯事） to do something wrong or illegal	**endure** [ɪn`djʊr] 忍受 to be in a difficult or painful situation without complaining
companion [kəm`pænjən] 同伴 a person you spend time with	**forecast** [for`kæst] 預測、預報 a description of what is about to happen in the future
departure [dɪ`partʃə] 離去、出發 the action of leaving a place, especially at the start of a journey	**fort** [fort] 堡壘、炮臺 a strong building used by soldiers or an army and is safeguarded from attack
digest [`daɪdʒɛst] 摘要、分類 to comprehend new information	**frequency** [`frikwənsɪ] 時常發生、頻率 something often occurs over a particular period of time
digital [`dɪdʒɪtl̩] 數字的、數位的 using a system in which information is sent out electronically in the form of num bers	**gallery** [`gælərɪ] 畫廊、美術館 a room where people can see pieces of art
discourage [dɪs`kɝɪdʒ] 阻止、妨礙 to persuade someone not to do something	**haste** [hest] 急忙、急速 in a hurry of action
disguise [dɪs`gaɪz] 喬裝、掩飾 to change the appearance of someone so that people can't recognize them	**hesitation** [ˌhɛzə`teʃən] 遲疑、躊躇 the act of hesitating

19

◉ 捷徑文化版權所有

◆用例句猜猜英文單字

ACROSS

2 Jesus used to help many people; it is no wonder that Jesus is believed by Christians to have been d___e.
5 A man driven by j___y is capable of anything, what do you think of that?
7 We forgot to pay the bill; it is no wonder that the electricity company has d___ted our electricity.
8 If you are lucky enough to spend vacation there, do you know what delights a___t you?
12 Lack of c___y is considered as a disease of modern society.
14 It will take you some time to a___t yourself with a new job.
15 Her ring was stolen. It is no wonder that she g___ed suspiciously at everyone got down from the plane.
16 His health c_____ed due to years of overwork.

DOWN

1 Let us d___s the topic and talk of something interesting.
3 Her mother was an actress. It is no wonder that she is so interested in pursuing a stage c___r.
4 Shouldn't you be ashamed of your foolish b___r, Tom?
6 Because there is so much unemployment, the c___n for jobs is fierce.
9 It is impossible for you to say with any a___y how many people are affected.
10 Do you mind buying some d___e instruments to these scientists?
11 I don't believe man will c___r the weather in the near future.
13 I don't think rights i___y duties; what about you?

◆上面的遊戲會用到的單字都在這裡！真的看不懂提示就來偷瞄一下吧！

WORD BANK: Accuracy, acquaint, await, behavior, career, collapse, competition, conquer, courtesy, delicate, disconnect, dismiss, divine, gaze, imply, jealousy.

答案就在後面

Level-3

◆填字遊戲解答在這裡！

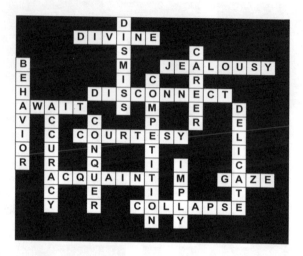

◆單字還記不熟嗎？快來做複習！

accuracy [ˈækjərəsɪ] 正確、精密 precision, the quality of being close to the true value	**courtesy** [ˈkɝtəsɪ] 禮貌、好意 politeness
acquaint [əˈkwent] 使熟悉、告知 to make someone familiar with something	**delicate** [ˈdɛləkət] 精細的、精巧的 very mild and fine in texture or structure
await [əˈwet] 等待 to wait for someone or something	**disconnect** [ˌdɪskəˈnɛkt] 斷絕、打斷 to interrupt
behavior [bɪˈhevjɚ] 舉止、行為 the way a person acts	**dismiss** [dɪsˈmɪs] 摒除、解散 to send away
career [kəˈrɪr] （終身的）職業、生涯 a job or profession which you do for a long period of life	**divine** [dəˈvaɪn] 神的、神聖的 relating to God or a god
collapse [kəˈlæps] 崩潰、倒塌 to fall down suddenly or give away	**gaze** [gez] 注視、凝視 to look steadily
competition [ˌkɑmpəˈtɪʃən] 競爭、競爭者 the action of competing against others especially in business or a sport	**imply** [ɪmˈplaɪ] 暗示、含有 to express or mean indirectly
conquer [ˈkɑŋkɚ] 征服 to get control of, to overcome	**jealousy** [ˈdʒɛləsɪ] 嫉妒 a feeling of upset because someone has something that you don't have

20

◉ 捷徑文化版權所有

◆用例句猜猜英文單字

ACROSS

1 Would you like to tell me how many c___es an ounce of sugar can supply?

4 Please send me your current c___e as soon as possible.

10 Not everyone knows that the e___y school is affiliated to that university.

13 This paly was excellent. It is no wonder that the audience roared in d___t.

14 Would you please help me find a good a___t?

15 Would you like to let me know if you got any c___e proposals?

16 Why not adopt the c___rs' suggestion? It will be helpful to you.

DOWN

2 I made the a___e of my husband at a party.

3 The infant finished his milk with a smile of c_____t.

5 Would you please schedule an a___t for me to meet with Mr. Liu?

6 Too much c___e can hurt you.

7 I prefer to have my hair in c___l; what about you?

8 I don't think the d___e can reason out how the murderer has escaped.

9 He has been studying very hard recently; it is no wonder that he can make r___e progress in his study quickly.

11 Don't you think these two ideas are quite d___t from each other?

12 It is the first time that she gives me a g___e of her true feelings.

◆上面的遊戲會用到的單字都在這裡！真的看不懂提示就來偷瞄一下吧！

WORD BANK: Accountant, acquaintance, appointment, calorie, concrete, confidence, consumer, contentment, curl, delight, detective, distinct, elementary, catalogue, glimpse, remarkable.

121

答案就在後面

◆填字遊戲解答在這裡！

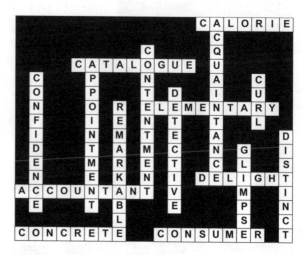

◆單字還記不熟嗎？快來做複習！

accountant [ə`kauntənt] 會計師 someone whose job is to keep or check financial accounts	**curl** [kɝl] 捲髮、捲曲 a piece of hair that hangs in a curved shape
acquaintance [ə`kwentəns] 認識的人、熟人 someone who is often seen and well known	**delight** [dɪ`laɪt] 欣喜 joy
appointment [ə`pɔɪntmənt] 指定、約定、指派、任用 an arrangement to meet or a job	**detective** [dɪ`tɛktɪv] 偵探、探員 a person whose job is to research crimes
calorie [`kælərɪ] 卡、卡路里 a unit for measuring the amount of energy that food offers	**distinct** [dɪ`stɪŋkt] 個別的、獨特的 unique or individual
concrete [`kɑnkrit] 水泥、混凝土、具體的 definite and specific	**elementary** [ˌɛlə`mɛntərɪ] 基本的、初級的 basic
confidence [`kɑnfədəns] 信心、信賴 firm belief; the fact of being or feeling certain	**catalogue** [`kætəlɔg] （圖書、商品）目錄 a systematic list of items
consumer [kən`sumɚ] 消費者 a person who buys and uses products and services	**glimpse** [glɪmps] 瞥見、隱約看見 to have a brief, quick view
contentment [kən`tɛntmənt] 滿足 a state of being satisfied	**remarkable** [rɪ`mɑrkəbl̩] 值得注意的 unusual, worthy of notice

122

21

◉ 捷徑文化版權所有

◆用例句猜猜英文單字

ACROSS

1 It is a surprise that the demonstration ended in a violent c___h with the police.
5 The more things you put in the b___k, the heavier it becomes.
7 I am afraid that I am not tactful enough to be a good d___t.
8 It is no wonder that she cannot learn that series of g___es. They are too difficult.
9 Susan is getting married; it is no wonder that I see her saying it with a f___h on her face.
10 I wish my son were an h___e man.
11 My chief a___t is reading novels.
12 This a___d is too strong. It is no wonder that it has burnt a hole in my jacket.
13 We are a___s to ensure that there is no misunderstanding between us.

DOWN

2 Why not pick up a dress a___e for the occasion?
3 He left for Hong Kong last month; it is no wonder that I haven't seen him l___y.
4 It was the f___t that damaged all the crops in the fields and plants by the road.
5 Have you seen the b___m in the car today? What does he look like?
6 The requirement of metal added a great quantity last year.It is no wonder that China's c___r imports increased by 80%last year.
8 He's in a good mood today; it is no wonder that he gave us a cheery g___g this morning.
9 I don't think his fiction has a large amount of f___y in it.

◆上面的遊戲會用到的單字都在這裡！真的看不懂提示就來偷瞄一下吧！

WORD BANK: Acid, amusement, anxious, appropriate, backpack, bridegroom, clash, copper, diplomat, fantasy, flush, frost, glide, greeting, honorable, lately.

答案就在後面

◆填字遊戲解答在這裡！

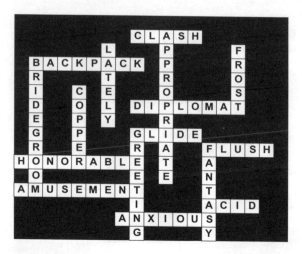

◆單字還記不熟嗎？快來做複習！

acid [ˈæsɪd] 酸性物質、酸的 a liquid substance which is capable of turning litmus red and reacting with a base to form a salt, sour	**diplomat** [ˈdɪpləmæt] 外交官 an official who represents their government in a foreign country
amusement [əˈmjuzmənt] 娛樂、有趣 a feeling of delight; the condition of being entertained	**fantasy** [ˈfæntəsɪ] 空想、異想 an idea or belief that is based only on imagination, not true
anxious [ˈæŋkʃəs] 憂心的、擔憂的 worried about something	**flush** [flʌʃ] 紅光、繁茂、沖洗 a red color that appears on your face
appropriate [əˈproprɪet] 適當的、適切的 proper or right for a specific situation	**frost** [frɔst] 霜、冷淡 the icy crystals that form directly on a freezing surface
backpack [ˈbækˌpæk] 背包 a rucksack worn on one's back	**glide** [glaɪd] 滑動、滑走、滑行 to move smoothly and easily
bridegroom [ˈbraɪdˌgrum] 新郎 a man who is about to be married or just after he is married	**greeting** [ˈgritɪŋ] 問候、問候語 something you say when you welcome someone
clash [klæʃ] 衝突、猛撞 an act or sound of clashing	**honorable** [ˈɑnərbl̩] 體面的、可敬的、高貴的 respectful, honest
copper [ˈkɑpɚ] 銅、銅製的 a red-brown metal that is used to make electrical wires	**lately** [ˈletlɪ] 最近 recently

22

◉ 捷徑文化版權所有

◆用例句猜猜英文單字

ACROSS

1 It is no wonder that the newspaper does not regard him as a good c___c.

3 How often do you go to the c___a with your family?

7 The design is quite novel. It is no wonder that it has such a strong v___l appeal.

10 There was d___e fog; it is no wonder that the traffic slowed down.

12 Why not make an a___n to the court for an inquiry?

13 I wish you weren't so c___l in the clothes you wear.

14 It was his foolish behavior that led to his e___l failure.

15 I am fond of reading all kinds of f___ns; what about you?

DOWN

2 There is no such thing as a good c___t.

3 I don't think you need to be so c___s to her.

4 It is no wonder that they could a___e anger among customers. It was too ridiculous.

5 Will you please give me some forms of i___n to prove yourself?

6 His honesty is beyond d___e, let's support him.

8 Do you know how to c___e music on the computer?

9 Not every person can master such a writing style in which every word is f___l.

11 He loves being a doctor. It is no wonder that he gave up e___g and took to medicine.

◆上面的遊戲會用到的單字都在這裡！真的看不懂提示就來偷瞄一下吧！

WORD BANK: Application, arouse, capitalist, cinema, compose, conventional, courteous, critic, dense, dispute, engineering, eventual, fiction, functional, identification, visual.

125

答案就在後面

◆填字遊戲解答在這裡！

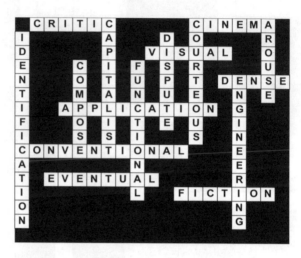

◆單字還記不熟嗎？快來做複習！

application [əˈplaɪəns] 請求、申請書、應用 a request for something like a job or place at university	**dense** [dɛns] 密集的、稠密的 made of a lot of things or people that are very close together
arouse [əˈraʊz] 喚醒、激起 to make someone become interested	**dispute** [dɪˈspjut] 爭論 to argue about something
capitalist [ˈkæpətlɪst] 資本家 an owner of wealth especially used in busines	**engineering** [ˌɛndʒəˈnɪrɪŋ] 工程學 the study concerned with the design, the use of machines and structures
cinema [ˈsɪnəmə] 電影院 a theater in which films are shown	**eventual** [ɪˈvɛntʃʊəl] 最後的 final, at last
compose [kəmˈpoz] 組成、作曲 to create, especially music or a literary work	**fiction** [ˈfɪkʃən] 小說、虛構 books about imaginary events and people
conventional [kənˈvɛnʃənl̩] 會議的、傳統的 based on convention	**functional** [ˈfʌŋkʃənl̩] 作用的、機能的 designed to be useful
courteous [ˈkɜtjəs] 有禮貌的 very kindly and gracious toward others	**identification** [aɪˌdɛntəfəˈkeʃən] 身分證、身分 an official document that proves who you are
critic [ˈkrɪtɪk] 批評家、評論的 someone whose job is to make judgments	**visual** [ˈvɪʒʊəl] 視覺的 relating to seeing

◉ 捷徑文化版權所有

◆用例句猜猜英文單字

ACROSS

1 It is no wonder that there were few a___ts for the job. The wages were too low.

3 Don't you think the b___d eagle in the forest is very horrible?

9 It's not necessary for you to worry about your g___r.

10 The air condition is getting worse; it is no wonder that they have taken measures to prevent e___t pollution.

11 There are plenty of n___y families in our village.

14 There is too great a consumption of a___l in China.

15 It takes courage and strength to climb these c___fs.

16 Neither you nor I can entirely keep away from this c___e world.

DOWN

2 Don't you think this is quite an a___s plan?

4 He is the boss; it is no wonder that all of them were caved in to his d___d.

5 It is quite clear that most people have a d___d of snakes.

6 It is clear that people still have a general fear for the i___y infernal powers.

7 Rainy weather always d___ses me and what's worse, I don't know what do to at home.

8 Why not f___h your own house according to your own taste?

12 Dynamite is a powerful e___e, don't you think so?

13 The king passed away very early. It is no wonder that the prince a___ed power when he was only fifteen.

◆上面的遊戲會用到的單字都在這裡！真的看不懂提示就來偷瞄一下吧！

WORD BANK: Alcohol, ambitious, applicant, assume, bald, cliff, competitive, demand, depress, dread, exhaust, explosive, furnish, grammar, imaginary, needy.

答案就在後面

◆填字遊戲解答在這裡！

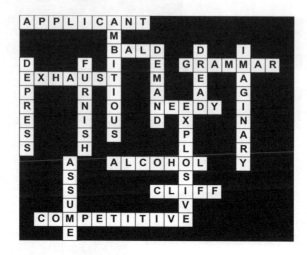

◆單字還記不熟嗎？快來做複習！

alcohol [ˈælkəˌhɔl] 酒精 a colorless volatile liquid compound such as beer or wine which can make people drunk	**depress** [dɪˈprɛs] 壓下、降低、使沮喪 to feel completely discouraged
ambitious [æmˈbɪʃəs] 雄心壯志的 determined to be successful	**dread** [drɛd] 非常害怕、敬畏、恐怖 a feeling of being frightened or worried
applicant [ˈæpləkənt] 申請人、應徵者 a person who requests or seeks something, such as a job	**exhaust** [ɪgˈzɔst] 耗盡 to make someone feel very tired
assume [əˈsum] 假定、擔任 to believe something to be true without evidence	**explosive** [ɪkˈsplosɪv] 炸藥、爆炸的 a substance that can cause an explosion
bald [bɔld] 禿頭的、禿的 having little or no hair	**furnish** [ˈfɝnɪʃ] 供給、裝備 to supply with furniture
cliff [klɪf] 峭壁、斷崖 a high, steep face of rock esp. on a coast	**grammar** [ˈgræmɚ] 文法 the rules about how words change their form and combine with other words to make sentences
competitive [kəmˈpɛtətɪv] 競爭的 based on or decided by competition	**imaginary** [ɪˈmædʒəˌnɛrɪ] 想像的、不實在的 not real or practical
demand [dɪˈmænd] 要求 to ask for something firmly	**needy** [ˈnidɪ] 貧窮的、貧困的、黏人的 very poor, having little food or money

24

◉ 捷徑文化版權所有

◆用例句猜猜英文單字

ACROSS

4 Tom was telling a joke; it's no wonder that there was a g___e from the back of the class.

5 Don't you know that the scientists have found the secret of the a___m?

8 It is helpful for you to begin with a rough and ready c___n.

10 Would you give me half an hour to c___e with you?

12 It took them two years to c___t the bridge.

14 Lightning usually a___ies thunder; don't you know that?

15 It is very difficult for the scientists to a___n an exact date to this building.

DOWN

1 It is a traditional way for people to c___e one's age

2 It is obvious that you should not walk on the wet c___t.

3 He is d___sing how to do that thing, so please don't disturb him.

6 I'm afraid that I can't c___e on my work when I'm tired.

7 It is obvious that it's not a matter of c___e but of choice.

9 It takes me half an hour to get to my d___y from the library.

10 As far as I know, there are five people living in that c___e.

11 Would you a___e the structure of the sentence for me?

13 Let us take part in the church c___s, ok?

◆上面的遊戲會用到的單字都在這裡！真的看不懂提示就來偷瞄一下吧！

WORD BANK: Accompany, analyze, assign, atom, calculate, cement, chorus, circumstance, classification, concentrate, construct, converse, cottage, devise, dormitory, giggle.

答案就在後面

◆填字遊戲解答在這裡！

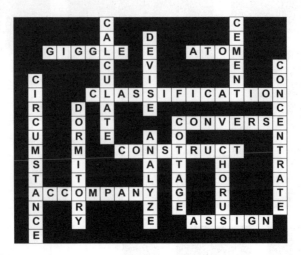

◆單字還記不熟嗎？快來做複習！

accompany [ə`kʌmpənɪ] 隨行、陪伴、伴隨 to go together with somebody	**classification** [ˌklæsəfə`keʃən] 分類 a process in which you put something into the group
analyze [`ænḷˌaɪz] 分析、解析 to think about or examine something carefully	**concentrate** [`kɑnsṇˌtret] 集中、全神貫注 to pay attention completely on something
assign [ə`saɪn] 分派、指定 to give someone a job	**construct** [kən`strʌkt] 建造、構築 to build something
atom [`ætəm] 原子 the smallest part of an element that can combine with other substances to form a mol	**converse** [kən`vɝs] 談話、交談 to have a conversation
calculate [`kælkjəˌlet] 計算 to count mathematically	**cottage** [`kɑtɪdʒ] 小屋 a small house, especially the one in the country
cement [sə`mɛnt] 水泥 a grey powder made from lime and clay, used in building	**devise** [dɪ`vaɪz] 裝置、設計、想出、策劃 to plan or contrive something
chorus [`korəs] 副歌、合唱團、合唱 a part of a song which is repeated many times after every verse; a group of people singing together	**dormitory** [`dɔrməˌtorɪ] 宿舍 a consist of many large rooms with many beds for students who can't commute in a school
circumstance [`sɝkəmˌstæns] 情況、環境 the conditions	**giggle** [`gɪgḷ] 咯咯地笑 to laugh with a series of uncontrollable high pitched sounds in a silly or nervous way

25

◉ 捷徑文化版權所有

◆用例句猜猜英文單字

ACROSS

3 I don't think the theory he put forward is d___e, do you agree?

5 Feminism works toward e_____y for all, women and men alike.

8 First of all, let's have a look at our a___o-visual classroom.

9 You will e___r your health if you work so hard; don't you think so?

12 Once we have gathered enough proofs, we can a___e him at the court.

13 Not all people can a___t themselves to the busy modern life in big cities.

14 The police sealed the whole area off so that no robber would f___e.

15 She has great f___y in learning languages, so does her brother.

16 Graduate school can offer the hope of an a_____c career.

DOWN

1 It is not easy for me to distinguish cultured pearls from g___e pearls.

2 We will hold a fire d___l this morning; would you like to come?

4 We are not sure about the number of survivors; it is no wonder that his e___e of the situation is not so optimistic.

6 You should know that there is no a___e standard for it.

7 They had a fight last night; it is no wonder that his wife was f___s with him.

10 The children lack d___e, and they are not old enough to understand the rules of the school.

11 He has killed many people before; it is no wonder that so many people are full of h___d for the man.

◆上面的遊戲會用到的單字都在這裡！真的看不懂提示就來偷瞄一下吧！

WORD BANK: Absolute, academic, accuse, adjust, audio, defensible, discipline, drill, endanger, equality, estimate, facility, flee, furious, genuine, hatred.

答案就在後面

Level-3

◆填字遊戲解答在這裡！

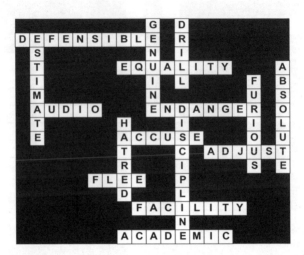

◆單字還記不熟嗎？快來做複習！

absolute [ˈæbsəˌlut] 絕對的 complete or total	**endanger** [ɪnˈdendʒɚ] 使陷入危險 to make something or someone in danger
academic [ˌækəˈdɛmɪk] 學院的、大學的 related to education and learning	**equality** [ɪˈkwɑlətɪ] 平等 a situation in which people have the same rights
accuse [əˈkjuz] 控告、譴責 to charge with a fault or offense	**estimate** [ˈɛstəmɪt] 評估 to try to guess the value of something without calculating it precisely
adjust [əˈdʒʌst] 調節、對準 to change slightly so as to complete the goal or a desired outcome	**facility** [fəˈsɪlətɪ] 容易、靈巧、能力 a natural ability to do something easily
audio [ˈɔdɪˌo] 聲音 the part of a recording that includes sounds	**flee** [fli] 逃走、逃避 to escape
defensible [dɪˈfɛnsəbl] 可辯護的、可防禦的 capable of being defended of protected	**furious** [ˈfjurɪəs] 狂怒的 very angry
discipline [ˈdɪsəplɪn] 紀律、訓練 a way of training people to obey rules	**genuine** [ˈdʒɛnjuɪn] 真正的、非假冒的 really being what it is; frank
drill [drɪl] 鑽、錐、鑽孔、演練 a tool or machine which is used for making holes	**hatred** [ˈhetrɪd] 怨恨、憎惡 a strong feeling of hate

26

◆用例句猜猜英文單字

ACROSS

1 It is clear that they show great anxiety concerning their retirement a___e.
3 This desgin is suitable for i___ts. don't you think so?
5 I felt very a___d and out of place at the formal ball.
6 I don't want to walk anymore; let's take the e___r.
10 How about this padded lace b___a? I think it fits you perfectly.
12 Would you like to tell me how much a c___r is in Britain?
13 Would you please buy two tickets for C___e No. 7 for us?
14 To save water is to c___h life, don't you know that?
15 There is an acknowledged e___s on equality for all.

DOWN

2 What a wonderful idea! We are all a___e to your proposal.
4 I wish I could understand such an a___t concept.
5 I enjoy reading Mark Twain's a___y; what about you?
7 It is quite clear that this man has been b___e since the last gambling.
8 I am afraid that my little son can't catch the ball on its first b___e.
9 He was a great emperor. It is no wonder that his death marked the end of an e___a.
11 I wish that meeting her in that coffee shop was purely a___l.

◆上面的遊戲會用到的單字都在這裡！真的看不懂提示就來偷瞄一下吧！

WORD BANK: Abstract, accidental, agreeable, allowance, autobiography, awkward, bounce, bra, broke, cape, cherish, cigar, emphasis, era, escalator, infant.

答案就在後面

◆填字遊戲解答在這裡！

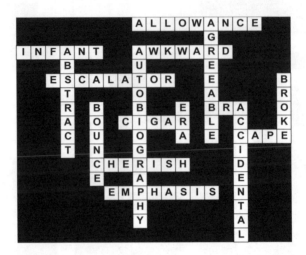

◆單字還記不熟嗎？快來做複習！

abstract [ˋæbstrækt] 抽象的 thought of apart from any particular instances or material objects, not concrete	**broke** [brok] 一無所有的、破產的 having no money, nothing left
accidental [ˌæksəˋdɛntḷ] 偶然的、意外的 happening without being planned, unexpected	**cape** [kep] 岬、海角 a large piece of land projecting into the sea
agreeable [əˋgriəbḷ] 令人愉快的、準備同意的 very pleasant	**cherish** [ˋtʃɛrɪʃ] 珍愛、珍惜 to care for tenderly or show love for
allowance [əˋlaʊəns] 津貼、補助 an amount of money that you are given regularly	**cigar** [sɪˋgɑr] 雪茄 a thin tube-shaped thing made from tobacco leaves for smoking
autobiography [ˌɔtəbaɪˋɑgrəfɪ] 自傳 a book that writes about one's life by oneself	**emphasis** [ˋɛmfəsɪs] 重點、強調 special importance or attention given to something by someone
awkward [ˋɔkwəd] 笨拙的、不熟練的 difficult to handle or manage	**era** [ˋɪrə] 時代 a period of time in history
bounce [baʊns] 彈、跳 to hit against a surface so as to rebound	**escalator** [ˋɛskəˌletə] 手扶梯 a set of moving staircase that take people to a different levels in a building
bra [brɑ] 胸罩、內衣 a piece of underwear worn by women to support the breasts	**infant** [ˋɪnfənt] 嬰兒 a baby

27

◉ 捷徑文化版權所有

◆用例句猜猜英文單字

ACROSS

2 The water is enough for a gardener to h___e this big garden.
4 Why not pass on the fine tradition of hard struggle from g___n to g___n?
9 The city hall is planning to start a c_____n against domestic violence.
10 Why not e___p yourself with a sharp pencil and an eraser for the exam?
13 I prefer c___y to physics.
14 There is no point in d___ring a war on such a weak country.
15 I'm afraid that it's too difficult for me to a___h the task alone.
16 It is hard for the farmers to get a harvest on these less f___e fields.

DOWN

1 In my opinion, there is no need to c___e the issue.
3 It is obvious that the failure was a great d___t to him, he lost his heart from then on.
5 It was Susan who won the spelling c___p.
6 I'm afraid it was a strange e___r that brought us together.
7 He was depressed by his d___t. I wish he could bounce back soon.
8 Do you mind my asking you a question about f___e?
11 Would you like a harbor tour on a f___y during holidays?
12 Roman was a mighty country; it is no wonder that the Roman E___e existed for several centuries.

◆上面的遊戲會用到的單字都在這裡！真的看不懂提示就來偷瞄一下吧！

WORD BANK: Accomplish, campaign, championship, chemistry, complicate, declare, defeat, discouragement, empire, encounter, equip, ferry, fertile, finance, generation, hose.

答案就在後面

◆填字遊戲解答在這裡！

◆單字還記不熟嗎？快來做複習！

accomplish [əˋkɑmplɪʃ] 達成、完成 to complete something successfully	empire [ˋɛmpaɪr] 帝國 a group of countries that are all controlled by a single person or government
campaign [kæmˋpen] 戰役、活動 a series of military or organized actions aimed to realize an objective in a particular region	encounter [ɪnˋkaʊntɚ] 遭遇 to meet someone without planning to
championship [ˋtʃæmpɪənˏʃɪp] 冠軍賽、冠軍 the position of being a champion	equip [ɪˋkwɪp] 裝備 to provide with the things that are needed for an intention
chemistry [ˋkɛmɪstrɪ] 化學 the science that is regarded with studying substances and the ways that they change	ferry [ˋfɛrɪ] 渡口、渡輪 a boat that carries people or goods across a river
complicate [ˋkɑmpləˏket] 使複雜 to make something more difficult to understand	fertile [ˋfɝtl] 肥沃的、豐富的 capable of producing a large number of crops
declare [dɪˋklɛr] 宣告、公告 to announce publicly	finance [faɪˋnæns] 財務、融資 the management of large amounts of money by government
defeat [dɪˋfit] 挫敗、擊敗、戰勝 to win a victory over someone in a competition	generation [ˏdʒɛnəˋreʃən] 世代 a group of individuals who are similar aged and sharing similar social experience
discouragement [dɪsˋkɝɪdʒmənt] 失望、氣餒 a feeling of losing confidence	hose [hoz] 水管、用軟管澆或洗 a piece of rubber or plastic which is used to direct water

28

◉ 捷徑文化版權所有

◆用例句猜猜英文單字

ACROSS

4 Not both sides are willing to take c___e attitudes on this issue.

7 I owe you an a___y for what I did last night; I hope you can forgive me.

11 Is there any up-to-date quality a___e manual?

12 There are a great many of cooking utensils made of a___m now.

13 Will you give us a d___n? We don't know how to use the machine.

14 She is interested in studying flowers; it is no wonder that she is k___n on growing flowers.

15 It took their daughter several years to understand the true cause of their d___e.

16 Would you please let us know if you don't wish our a___t to call?

DOWN

1 I will never do anything g___y, don't you believe me?

2 There must be a___e room for people to gather.

3 Not every woman a___es happiness with having money.

5 Why not d___e the lands to the peasants?

6 Happiness is not a reward but a c___e, don't you agree?

8 My sister is f___e enough to win the first prize in the speech contest.

9 A computer is a d___e for processing information; the more you use it, the more you know.

10 Would you please tell me how he a___ed his wealth?

◆上面的遊戲會用到的單字都在這裡！真的看不懂提示就來偷瞄一下吧！

WORD BANK: Acquire, adequate, agent, aluminum, apology, associate, assurance, consequence, cooperative, demonstration, device, distribute, divorce, fortunate, guilty, keen.

答案就在後面

◆填字遊戲解答在這裡！

```
                                       G           A
                                       U           D
           A               C O O P E R A T I V E   Q
  D        S                       C   L           U
  I        S           A P O L O G Y   T           A
  S        O     F             N   A   Y           T
  T        C     O             S   D   A           E
  R        I   A S S U R A N C E   E   C
  B        A     T             Q   V   Q
  U        T     U       A L U M I N U M
  T        E     N             E   C   I
D E M O N S T R A T I O N     E       R
                 T             C       K E E N
    D I V O R C E       A G E N T
```

◆單字還記不熟嗎？快來做複習！

acquire [əˋkwaɪr] 取得、獲得 to get or obtain	**cooperative** [koˋɑpəˏretɪv] 合作的 willing to work together
adequate [ˋædəkwɪt] 適當的、足夠的 sufficient or acceptable	**demonstration** [ˏdɛmənˋstreʃən] 證明、示範 the action of explaining or showing how something works
agent [ˋedʒənt] 代理人、特工 a person who offers a specific information, especially in business	**device** [dɪˋvaɪs] 裝置、設計 a machine or tool that has a particular purpose
aluminum [əˋlumɪnəm] 鋁 a silvery ductile metallic element found primarily in bauxite	**distribute** [dɪˋstrɪbjut] 分配、分發 to give something out to people
apology [əˋpɑlədʒɪ] 謝罪、道歉 an act of saying sorry	**divorce** [dəˋvors] 離婚 to end a marriage
associate [əˋsoʃɪɪt] 聯合 to make a connection between one thing and another	**fortunate** [ˋfɔrtʃənɪt] 幸運的、僥倖的 very lucky
assurance [əˋʃurəns] 保證、保險 a promise that something is apparently true	**guilty** [ˋgɪltɪ] 有罪的、內疚的 feeling ashamed because you know that you have done something wrong
consequence [ˋkɑnsəˏkwɛns] 結果 outcome	**keen** [kin] 熱心的、敏銳的 eager to do something; enthusiastic

MID CAMPUS FORTUNE JUNIOR

29

◉ 捷徑文化版權所有

◆用例句猜猜英文單字

ACROSS

1 The situation poses a g___e threat to peace.
4 I won't a___e unless she admits her mistake first.
5 Don't you think that the first walk on the moon was quite an a___t?
7 It's too hard for me to move this piano without a___e.
8 Once you always e___e, people will no longer believe you.
12 It's four days before a very big i___g floated towards the Titanic.
13 My dream is to reach every corner of the g___e; what about you?
14 We are too heavily committed to be able to e___n new orders.
15 Will you change the baby's d___r? I am a bit busy now.

DOWN

2 Would you like to help me write an e___y in English?
3 I don't think it's necessary for you to c___t him first.
6 This kind of tea acts as an aid to d___n; why not have a try?
7 The doctor a___ted me for the danger of a heart attack.
9 Would you please e___e the address proof dated within the latest three months?
10 There is perfect h___y between the husband and the wife.
11 It's still hard for me to tell who will e___e victorious.

◆上面的遊戲會用到的單字都在這裡！真的看不懂提示就來偷瞄一下吧！

WORD BANK: Accomplishment, alert, apologize, assistance, consult, diaper, digestion, emerge, enclose, entertain, essay, exaggerate, globe, grave, harmony, iceberg.

139

答案就在後面

Level-3

◆填字遊戲解答在這裡！

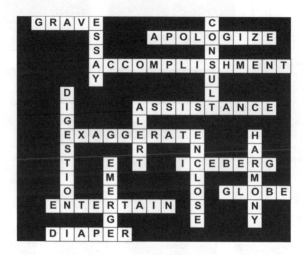

◆單字還記不熟嗎？快來做複習！

accomplishment [ə`kɑmplɪʃmənt] 達成、完成、才藝 a success; an ability that has been obtained by training	**enclose** [ɪn`kloz] 包圍 to surround something in order to make it separate
alert [ə`lɝt] 機警的、警戒 watchful and ready, as in facing danger	**entertain** [ˌɛntɚ`ten] 招待、娛樂 to amuse people in a way that gives them enjoyment
apologize [ə`pɑləˌdʒaɪz] 道歉、認錯 to ask for forgiveness	**essay** [`ɛse] 短文、隨筆 a short writing about a particular subject
assistance [ə`sɪstəns] 幫助、援助 help or support	**exaggerate** [ɪg`zædʒɚˌret] 誇大 to overstate, to make something look better, worse etc than it is
consult [kən`sʌlt] 請教、諮詢 to search information or advice from someone with special knowledge	**globe** [glob] 地球、球 the earth
diaper [`daɪəpɚ] 尿布 a baby's nappy	**grave** [grev] 墓穴、填墓、重大的 a hole in the ground to bury a dead body
digestion [də`dʒɛstʃən] 消化、消化作用 the process of digesting	**harmony** [`hɑrmənɪ] 一致、和諧 a state of completing agreement; a combination of parts into a pleasing or orderly whole
emerge [ɪ`mɝdʒ] 浮現 to appear from somewhere	**iceberg** [`aɪsˌbɝg] 冰山 a large mass of ice floating in the sea

140

30

◉ 捷徑文化版權所有

◆用例句猜猜英文單字

ACROSS

2 Would you like to tell me how many e___ds you will do in the business trip?

7 Don't you remember that next Monday is the a___y of when we first met?

8 It was the p___t, Sigmund Freud, who put forward a theory and shocked the entire world.

12 There is an a___n of the poet's work in the book.

13 Would you tell me why the President lost the support of the c___s?

15 It is no wonder that this car is e___l to run because it doesn't use much fuel.

16 What do you think about discussing the problem in c___l?

DOWN

1 It is the a___e that is used to describe or add to the meaning of a noun.

3 Why not invite him to the f___t? He once was your best friend.

4 It is obvious that he is i___t of what happened.

5 Don't you think that the satellite has become an important means of c___n?

6 Don't talk with her about this, or that will bring a b___h into her cheeks.

9 I think it's time for me to c___s the whole thing.

10 There were some a___l flowers on the table; do you like them?

11 I don't think that she has good g___es from her parents.

14 Will you help me hang my coat on the h___k, Susan?

◆上面的遊戲會用到的單字都在這裡！真的看不懂提示就來偷瞄一下吧！

WORD BANK: Adjective, anniversary, appreciation, artificial, blush, communication, confess, congress, council, economical, errand, feast, gene, hook, ignorant, psychologist.

答案就在後面

◆填字遊戲解答在這裡！

Crossword grid answers:

```
              A
      E R R A N D      F
                       E        I
  C   B   A N N I V E R S A R Y  G
  O   L   C           S          N
  M   U   T           T          O
  M P S Y C H O L O G I S T      R
  U   H   I           A          A
  N   G   O   A P P R E C I A T I O N
  I   E   N           I          T
  C O N G R E S S   H I F
  A   E   S         E C O N O M I C A L
  T       S         O   I
  I                 O   C
  O                 K   I
  N           C O U N C I L
                        A
```

◆單字還記不熟嗎？快來做複習！

adjective [ˈædʒɪktɪv] 形容詞 a word that describes a noun	**council** [ˈkaʊnsl̩] 議會、會議 a formal meeting with people who chosen to give advice
anniversary [ˌænəˈvɜˑsərɪ] 周年紀念日、結婚週年 an annually recurring date on which some event took place	**economical** [ˌikəˈnɑmɪkl̩] 節儉的 using money carefully without wasting any
appreciation [əˌpriʃɪˈeʃən] 賞識、鑑識 recognition of the value of something	**errand** [ˈɛrənd] 任務、差事 a short trip made to carry a message or do a definite thing
artificial [ˌɑrtəˈfɪʃəl] 人工的 something made to be like something that is real or natural	**feast** [fist] 宴會、節日 a well-prepared meal
blush [blʌʃ] 臉紅 to become red in the face from shame of embarrassment	**gene** [dʒin] 基因、遺傳因子 a part of a cell in a living thing that controls what it looks like, and how it develops
communication [kəˌmjunəˈkeʃən] 通信、溝通、交流 ways of exchanging information or expressing feelings and thoughts	**hook** [hʊk] 鉤、鉤子 a piece of curved metal used for catching fish or hanging things on
confess [kənˈfɛs] 承認、供認 to admit a crime or fault	**ignorant** [ˈɪgnərənt] 缺乏教育的、無知的 showing lack of knowledge or education
congress [ˈkɑngrəs] 國會 a formal meeting of representatives of societies, especially to exchange information	**psychologist** [saɪˈkɑlədʒɪst] 心理學家 a person who is trained in psychology

THE END OF THIS LEVEL

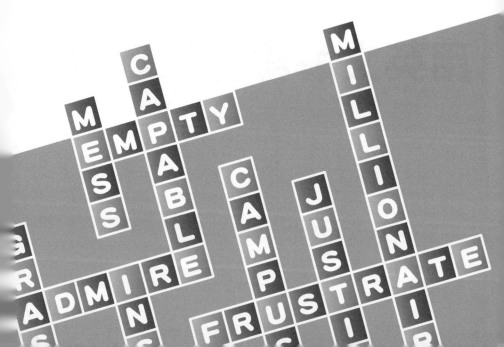

Level

用英文解釋提示玩單字

1

◉ 捷徑文化版權所有

◆用英文解釋猜猜英文單字

ACROSS

3 to make (opinions, feeling, information, etc.) known or understood by others
8 an action
9 a rodent with a long bushy tail, which climbs trees and feeds on nuts
13 to make an answer
14 benefit
15 a thought to believe that something is true; to think that someone's words is true
16 the area which is outside cities and near farms or woods

DOWN

1 to make able
2 a small drop which forms during night time
4 to come to an end
5 a club where people dance to recorded popular music
6 an necessary item; a required quality
7 hardworking
10 to affect; the power to have an effect on people or things
11 to astonish
12 a rough path or minor road; to follow the movements

◆上面的遊戲會用到的單字都在這裡！真的看不懂提示就來偷瞄一下吧！

WORD BANK: Advantage, amaze, belief, communicate, conclude, countryside, deed, dew, diligent, disco, enable, influence, requirement, reply, squirrel, track.

答案就在後面

◆填字遊戲解答在這裡！

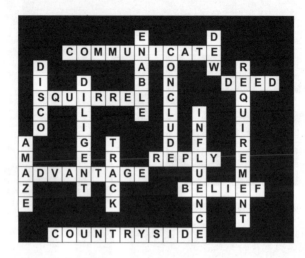

◆單字還記不熟嗎？快來做複習！

advantage [əd`væntɪdʒ] 利益、優勢 benefit	**diligent** [`dɪlədʒənt] 勤勉的、勤奮的 hardworking
amaze [ə`mez] 吃驚 to astonish	**disco** [`dɪsko] 迪斯可、小舞廳 a club where people dance to recorded popular music
belief [bɪ`lif] 相信、信念 a thought to believe that something is true; to think that someone's words is true	**enable** [ɪn`ebl] 使能夠 to make able
communicate [kə`mjunəˌket] 溝通、交流 to make (opinions, feeling, information, etc.) known or understood by others	**influence** [`ɪnfluəns] 影響 to affect; the power to have an effect on people or things
conclude [kən`klud] 結束 to come to an end	**requirement** [rɪ`kwaɪrmənt] 需要 an necessary item; a required quality
countryside [`kʌntrɪˌsaɪd] 鄉間 the area which is outside cities and near farms or woods	**reply** [rɪ`plaɪ] 回答、答覆 to make an answer
deed [did] 行為、行動 an action	**squirrel** [`skwɜ·əl] 松鼠 a rodent with a long bushy tail, which climbs trees and feeds on nuts
dew [dju] 露水 a small drop which forms during night time	**track** [træk] 路線 a rough path or minor road; to follow the movements

2

◉ 捷徑文化版權所有

◆用英文解釋猜猜英文單字

ACROSS

5 full of power
6 able to be moved
7 a person who is listening; the audience
9 sleepy
10 a hollow passage often rising above the roof of a building which allows smoke and gases to pass from a fire
12 the event of discovering
13 a small stream

DOWN

1 to put in or into a liquid for a moment
2 able to be measured
3 of or within a particular country / family
4 to ask for someone to help
7 a destruction; a ruin
8 a part of plants that grows leaves or fruits; a small shop of one large enterprise
10 a person who is afraid to face danger, pain, or hardship
11 very tidy or well arranged
12 to fall or let fall in drops

◆上面的遊戲會用到的單字都在這裡！真的看不懂提示就來偷瞄一下吧！

WORD BANK: Beg, branch, brook, chimney, coward, dip, discovery, domestic, drip, drowsy, listener, loss, movable, neat, measurable, powerful.

147

◆填字遊戲解答在這裡！

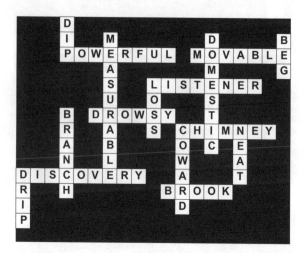

◆單字還記不熟嗎？快來做複習！

beg [bɛg] 乞討、懇求 to ask for someone to help	**drip** [drɪp] 滴、水滴 to fall or let fall in drops
branch [bræntʃ] 分支 a part of plants that grows leaves or fruits; a small shop of one large enterprise	**drowsy** [ˋdrauzɪ] 沉寂的、懶洋洋的、睏的 sleepy
brook [bruk] 川、小河、溪流 a small stream	**listener** [ˋlɪsn̩ɚ] 聽眾、聽者 a person who is listening; the audience
chimney [ˋtʃɪmnɪ] 煙囪 a hollow passage often rising above the roof of a building which allows smoke and gases to pass from a fire	**loss** [lɔs] 損失 a destruction; a ruin
coward [ˋkauɚd] 懦夫、膽子小的人 a person who is afraid to face danger, pain, or hardship	**movable** [ˋmuvəbl̩] 可移動的 able to be moved
dip [dɪp] 浸泡、傾斜、下沉 to put in or into a liquid for a moment	**neat** [nit] 整潔的 very tidy or well arranged
discovery [dɪˋskʌvɚɪ] 發現 the event of discovering	**measurable** [ˋmɛʒərəbl̩] 可測量的 able to be measured
domestic [dəˋmɛstɪk] 國內的、家務的 of or within a particular country/family	**powerful** [ˋpauɚfəl] 有力的 full of power

3

◉ 捷徑文化版權所有

◆用英文解釋猜猜英文單字

ACROSS

3 a kind of cloth used to keep one clean while one is cooking
4 a town or city with a harbor
6 occasional
10 to try very hard for a purpose
11 the official spoken language of Chinese
12 a kind of sticky material which is usually used for pottery or bricks
13 able to do things well
15 the fact or state of being independent

DOWN

1 a judgment or decision reached after consideration
2 to advice; to give a suggestion; to ask someone to marry you
4 a person who takes photographs
5 to hit or knock against with force or violence
7 a passenger vehicle
8 severly desciplined
9 able to attract
14 fearless, daring

◆上面的遊戲會用到的單字都在這裡！真的看不懂提示就來偷瞄一下吧！

WORD BANK: Apron, attractive, automobile, bold, bump, capable, casual, clay, conclusion, independence, mandarin, photographer, propose, port, strict, struggle.

149

◆填字遊戲解答在這裡！

◆單字還記不熟嗎？快來做複習！

apron [ˈeprən] 圍裙 a kind of cloth used to keep one clean while one is cooking	**conclusion** [kənˈkluʒən] 結論 a judgment or decision reached after consideration
attractive [əˈtræktɪv] 吸引人的、動人的 able to attract	**independence** [ˌɪndɪˈpɛndəns] 自立、獨立 the fact or state of being independent
automobile [ˈɔtəməˌbil] 汽車 a passenger vehicle	**mandarin** [ˈmændərɪn] 國語 the official spoken language of Chinese
bold [bold] 大膽的 fearless, daring	**photographer** [fəˈtɑgrəfɚ] 攝影師 a person who takes photographs
bump [bʌmp] 碰、撞 to hit or knock against with force or violence	**propose** [prəˈpoz] 提議、求婚 to advice; to give a suggestion; to ask someone to marry you
capable [ˈkepəbl̩] 有能力的 able to do things well	**port** [port] 港口 a town or city with a harbor
casual [ˈkæʒuəl] 偶然的、臨時的、輕便的 occasional	**strict** [strɪkt] 嚴格的 severely disciplined
clay [kle] 黏土 a kind of sticky material which is usually used for pottery or bricks	**struggle** [ˈstrʌgl̩] 努力、奮鬥 to try very hard for a purpose

4

◉ 捷徑文化版權所有

◆用英文解釋猜猜英文單字

ACROSS

2 relating to the army or war
3 to tie something
4 to make firmly fixed
9 to stop someone from committing crimes by police officers
10 a state or situation
12 pressure put on something that can make it lose its shape; to emphasize
13 something, especially a prize or money, given as the result of an official decision
15 the sort of food and drink usually taken by a person or group

DOWN

1 a thin paper tube of finely cut tobacco for smoking
3 anything that is carried; load
5 not wearing any clothes; completed bare
6 a covering of leather or rubber for the foot and ankel, usually heavier and thicker than a shoe
7 small living things which can cause illness
8 the person who has a lot of knowledge in the bank field
11 a long narrow channel dug to hold or carry water
14 to throw oneself head first into water

◆上面的遊戲會用到的單字都在這裡！真的看不懂提示就來偷瞄一下吧！

WORD BANK: Arrest, award, bacteria, banker, bind, boot, burden, cigarette, condition, diet, ditch, dive, fasten, naked, military, stress.

Level-4

◆填字遊戲解答在這裡！

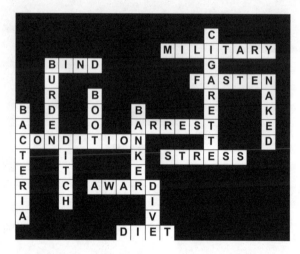

◆單字還記不熟嗎？快來做複習！

arrest [əˋrɛst] 逮捕、拘捕 to stop someone from committing crimes by police officers	**condition** [kənˋdɪʃən] 條件、情況 a state or situation
award [əˋwɔrd] 授與、頒獎 something, especially a prize or money, given as the result of an official decision	**diet** [ˋdaɪət] 節食 the sort of food and drink usually taken by a person or group
bacteria [bækˋtɪrɪə] 細菌 small living things which can cause illness	**ditch** [dɪtʃ] 挖溝、擺脫、拋棄 a long narrow channel dug to hold or carry water
banker [ˋbæŋkɚ] 銀行家 the person who has a lot of knowledge in the bank field	**dive** [daɪv] 跳水、潛心於 to throw oneself head first into water
bind [baɪnd] 綁、包紮 to tie something	**fasten** [ˋfæsn̩] 緊固、繫緊 to make firmly fixed
boot [but] 長靴 a covering of leather or rubber for the foot and ankel, usually heavier and thicker than a shoe	**naked** [ˋnekɪd] 裸露的、赤裸的 not wearing any clothes; completed bare
burden [ˋbɝdn̩] 負荷、負擔 anything that is carried; load	**military** [ˋmɪləˌtɛrɪ] 軍事、軍隊 relating to the army or war
cigarette [ˋsɪgəˌrɛt] 香煙 a thin paper tube of finely cut tobacco for smoking	**stress** [strɛs] 壓力、著重 pressure put on something that can make it lose its shape; to emphasize

152

5

◉ 捷徑文化版權所有

◆用英文解釋猜猜英文單字

ACROSS

3 the desire of eating
5 to ask for something for temporary use
6 the soft grey powder that remains after something has been burnt
8 to make someone understand something
12 equivalent in value ot the sum or itme specified
13 a type of shot fired from a fairly small gun
14 being unable to see things
15 to set a particular position in order to be picturized
16 the way to tell the correst sequences of the letters of a word

DOWN

1 to run quickly, esp. when hurrying
2 to fail to fulfill the hopes of a person
4 a group of people chosen, especially by and from a larger group, to do a particular job or for special duties
7 resolution; the answer to a problem
9 uncertain
10 any person who
11 to slide a short distance accidentally which makes you almost fall

◆上面的遊戲會用到的單字都在這裡！真的看不懂提示就來偷瞄一下吧！

WORD BANK: Appetite, ash, awaken, blind, borrow, bullet, committee, dash, disappoint, doubtful, pose, slip, solution, spelling, whoever, worth.

答案就在後面

◆填字遊戲解答在這裡！

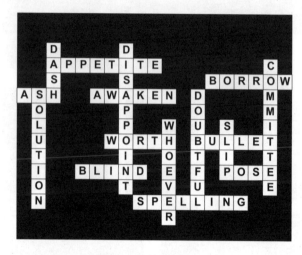

◆單字還記不熟嗎？快來做複習！

appetite [ˋæpəˏtaɪt] 食欲、胃口 the desire of eating	**disappoint** [ˏdɪsəˋpɔɪnt] 使失望 to fail to fulfill the hopes of a person
ash [æʃ] 灰燼、灰 the soft grey powder that remains after something has been burnt	**doubtful** [ˋdautfəl] 有疑問的、可疑的 uncertain
awaken [əˋwekən] 使……覺悟 to make someone understand something	**pose** [poz] 姿勢 to set a particular position in order to be pasteurized
blind [blaɪnd] 瞎的 being unable to see things	**slip** [slɪp] 滑倒 to slide a short distance accidentally which makes you almost fall
borrow [ˋbaro] 借、採用 to ask for something for temporary use	**solution** [səˋluʃən] 溶解、解決、解釋 resolution; the answer to a problem
bullet [ˋbulɪt] 子彈、彈頭 a type of shot fired from a fairly small gun	**spelling** [ˋspɛlɪŋ] 拼讀、拼法 the way to tell the correct sequences of the letters of a word
committee [kəˋmɪtɪ] 委員會、會議 a group of people chosen, especially by and from a larger group, to do a particular job or for special duties	**whoever** [huˋɛvɚ] 任何人、無論誰 any person who
dash [dæʃ] 碰撞、投擲 to run quickly, esp. when hurrying	**worth** [wɝθ] 價值 equivalent in value to the sum or item specified

6

◉ 捷徑文化版權所有

◆用英文解釋猜猜英文單字

ACROSS

3 in spite of the point that one just mentioned
4 let in, to permit to enter
5 a kind of seats that is long enough for two or more people to sit on
6 to show or perform something
8 something round on your waist to make your pants fit your body
9 to teach or train
10 the goals in one's life or in a period of life
11 a glass container for fish and other water animals
12 hair that grows around one's chin or cheeks
13 a ciminal who is kept in prison

DOWN

1 full of grass; covered with grass
2 a person who creates
4 a kind of chairs with arms and is comfortable to sit in
6 to damage something so severely that it cannot be repaired
7 a person whose job is to give advice
9 the choosing by vote of a representative to take an official position

◆上面的遊戲會用到的單字都在這裡！真的看不懂提示就來偷瞄一下吧！

WORD BANK: Admit, adviser, anyway, aquarium, armchair, beard, belt, bench, creator, destroy, display, educate, election, grassy, prisoner, target.

答案就在後面

◆填字遊戲解答在這裡！

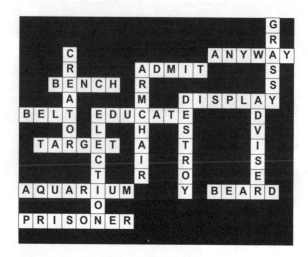

◆單字還記不熟嗎？快來做複習！

admit [ədˋmɪt] 容許……進入、承認 let in, to permit to enter	**creator** [krɪˋetɚ] 創造者、創作家 a person who creates
adviser [ədˋvaɪzɚ] 顧問 a person whose job is to give advice	**destroy** [dɪˋstrɔɪ] 損毀、毀壞 to damage something so severely that it cannot be repaired
anyway [ˋɛnɪ͵we] 無論如何 in spite of the point that one just mentioned	**display** [dɪˋsple] 展示、展覽 to show or perform something
aquarium [əˋkwɛrɪəm] 水族館 a glass container for fish and other water animals	**educate** [ˋɛdʒə͵ket] 教育 to teach or train
armchair [ˋɑrm͵tʃɛr] 扶椅 a kind of chairs with arms and is comfortable to sit in	**election** [ɪˋlɛkʃən] 選舉 the choosing by vote of a representative to take an official position
beard [bɪrd] 鬍子 hair that grows around one's chin or cheeks	**grassy** [ˋgræsɪ] 多草的 full of grass; covered with grass
belt [bɛlt] 皮帶 something round on your waist to make your pants fit your body	**prisoner** [ˋprɪzṇɚ] 囚犯 a criminal who is kept in prison
bench [bɛntʃ] 長凳 a kind of seats that is long enough for two or more people to sit on	**target** [ˋtɑrgɪt] 目標、靶子 the goals in one's life or in a period of life

7

◆用英文解釋猜猜英文單字

ACROSS

2 the limit in a certain extent; a line or a series
4 a woman about to be married
6 to lose blood
8 an individual thing
9 a person who wears funny clothing and exaggerated make-up to make people laugh
10 worth having, doing, or desiring
12 a group of words without a finite verb; to express with words
14 a long, narrow valley between high cliffs, usually with a river flowing through it
15 a number or numerical symbol

DOWN

1 a kind of weapons with one sharp point at one end; a sign used to show direction
3 the ruler of an empire
4 a kind of unpleasant tastes which is similar to black coffee; unpleasant
5 to inspire someone not to give up
7 a nocturnal bird with a flat face, large eyes, and strong curved nails
11 one of the most important organs of human beings, which controls our mind, sensation and every movement
13 the beginning or the origin

◆上面的遊戲會用到的單字都在這裡！真的看不懂提示就來偷瞄一下吧！

WORD BANK: Arrow, bitter, bleed, brain, bride, canyon, clown, desirable, emperor, encourage, figure, item, owl, phrase, range, source.

答案就在後面

◆填字遊戲解答在這裡！

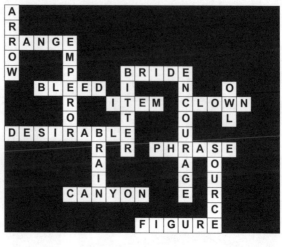

◆單字還記不熟嗎？快來做複習！

arrow [ˋæro] 箭 a kind of weapons with one sharp point at one end; a sign used to show direction	**emperor** [ˋɛmpərɚ] 皇帝 the ruler of an empire
bitter [ˋbɪtɚ] 苦的、嚴厲的 a kind of unpleasant tastes which is similar to black coffee; unpleasant	**encourage** [ɪnˋkɝɪdʒ] 鼓勵 to inspire someone not to give up
bleed [blid] 流血 to lose blood	**figure** [ˋfɪgjɚ] 人影、畫像、數字 a number or numerical symbol
brain [bren] 腦、智力 one of the most important organs of human beings, which controls our mind, sensation and every movement	**item** [ˋaɪtəm] 項目、條款 an individual thing
bride [braɪd] 新娘 a woman about to be married	**owl** [aʊl] 貓頭鷹 a nocturnal bird with a flat face, large eyes, and strong curved nails
canyon [ˋkænjən] 峽谷 a long, narrow valley between high cliffs, usually with a river flowing through it	**phrase** [frez] 片語 a group of words without a finite verb; to express with words
clown [klaʊn] 小丑 a person who wears funny clothing and exaggerated make-up to make people laugh	**range** [rendʒ] 範圍 the limit in a certain extent; a line or a series
desirable [dɪˋzaɪrəbl̩] 值得的、稱心如意的 worth having, doing, or desiring	**source** [sors] 來源、水源地 the beginning or the origin

8

◆用英文解釋猜猜英文單字

ACROSS

1 to gamble on something
4 the state that someone is not at present; the person you visit is out
6 a wide opening along a coast
7 a thief who breaks into houses, shops, etc. with the intention of stealing, esp. during the night
8 made of wood
11 to arrange for something to happen
14 an invitation to compete in a fight, match, etc.
15 to arrange to employ someone

DOWN

2 a number of copies of a book, newspaper, magazine, etc., that are produced and printed at one time
3 transportation
5 of, related to, or used in commerce
8 happy to do
9 the arch or line of short hair growing above the eye
10 adolescence; the period of teen years
12 to crush or keep biting with the teeth
13 owed or owing as a debt

◆上面的遊戲會用到的單字都在這裡！真的看不懂提示就來偷瞄一下吧！

WORD BANK: Absence, bay, bet, burglar, carriage, challenge, chew, commercial, due, edition, engage, eyebrow, organize, teenage, willing, wooden.

答案就在後面

◆填字遊戲解答在這裡！

◆單字還記不熟嗎？快來做複習！

absence [ˈæbsn̩s] 缺席 the state that someone is not at present; the person you visit is out	**due** [dju] 應付款、欠的 owed or owing as a debt
bay [be] 海灣 a wide opening along a coast	**edition** [əˈdɪʃən] 版本 a number of copies of a book, newspaper, magazine, etc., that are produced and printed at one time
bet [bɛt] 打賭 to gamble on something	**engage** [ɪnˈgedʒ] 僱用、允諾、訂婚、從事 to arrange to employ someone
burglar [ˈbɝglɚ] 夜盜、竊賊 a thief who breaks into houses, shops, etc. with the intention of stealing, esp. during the night	**eyebrow** [ˈaɪˌbraʊ] 眉毛 the arch or line of short hair growing above the eye
carriage [ˈkærɪdʒ] 車輛、車、馬車 transportation	**organize** [ˈɔrgəˌnaɪz] 組織、系統化 to arrange for something to happen
challenge [ˈtʃælɪndʒ] 挑戰 an invitation to compete in a fight, match, etc.	**teenage** [ˈtinˌedʒ] 十幾歲的、青少年時期 adolescence; the period of teen years
chew [tʃu] 咀嚼 to crush or keep biting with the teeth	**willing** [ˈwɪlɪŋ] 心甘情願的、願意的 happy to do
commercial [kəˈmɝʃəl] 商業的 of, related to, or used in commerce	**wooden** [ˈwʊdn̩] 木製的 made of wood

9

Level-4

◆用英文解釋猜猜英文單字

ACROSS

2 the upper front part of the body between the neck and the stomach, enclosing the heart and lungs
8 a kind of bugs with hard back; to rush to somewhere
9 viewpoint on something
11 over or to cross a state
12 a large wild animal of the cat family from African or Southern Asia, usually tawny with black spots
13 the cabinet in a house for keeping books
16 an insect with a long thin body, a large head, large eyes and two pairs of transparent wings outstretched at rest

DOWN

1 specific; unique
3 a piece of clothing fastened around the waist and hanging down around the legs
4 a puppet which looks like a person or an animal and you can direct it acts by strings
5 talks between two or more people as a feature of a book, play or film
6 the connection between two things or two people
7 a set of things that is tied together
10 a plan adjusting expenses during a certain period to the estimated income for that period
14 to give an emergency help; to help others
15 to curve something or to move one's body to make it not straight

◆上面的遊戲會用到的單字都在這裡！真的看不懂提示就來偷瞄一下吧！

WORD BANK: Aid, attitude, beetle, bend, beyond, bookcase, budget, bundle, chest, dialogue, dragonfly, leopard, particular, puppet, relation, skirt.

答案就在後面

◆填字遊戲解答在這裡！

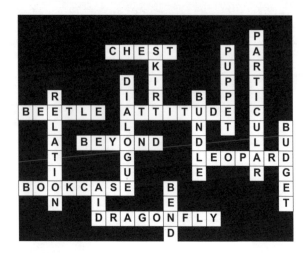

◆單字還記不熟嗎？快來做複習！

aid [ed] 幫助、支援 to give an emergency help; to help others	**chest** [tʃɛst] 胸、箱子 the upper front part of the body between the neck and the stomach, enclosing the heart and lungs
attitude [ˈætətjʊd] 態度、心態、看法 viewpoint on something	**dialogue** [ˈdaɪəˌlɔg] 對話 talks between two or more people as a feature of a book, play or film
beetle [ˈbitl̩] 甲蟲、急忙走 a kind of bugs with hard back; to rush to somewhere	**dragonfly** [ˈdrægənˌflaɪ] 蜻蜓 an insect with a long thin body, a large head, large eyes and two pairs of transparent wings outstretched at rest
bend [bɛnd] 使彎曲 to curve something or to move one's body to make it not straight	**leopard** [ˈlɛpəd] 豹 a large wild animal of the cat family from African or Southern America, usually tawny with black spots
beyond [brˈjɑnd] 越過 over or to cross a state	**particular** [pəˈtɪkjələ] 特別的 specific; unique
bookcase [ˈbʊkˌkes] 書櫃、書架 the cabinet in a house for keeping books	**puppet** [ˈpʌpɪt] 木偶、傀儡 a puppet which looks like a person or an animal and you can direct it acts by strings
budget [ˈbʌdʒɪt] 預算 a plan adjusting expenses during a certain period to the estimated income for that period	**relation** [rɪˈleʃən] 關係 the connection between two things or two people
bundle [ˈbʌndl̩] 捆、包裹 a set of things that is tied together	**skirt** [skɝt] 裙子 a piece of clothing fastened around the waist and hanging down around the legs

10

◉ 捷徑文化版權所有

◆用英文解釋猜猜英文單字

ACROSS

3 a piece of furniture with doors, or a set of shelves with doors, where clothes, plates, food, etc., can be stored

5 the power or ability to please, attract or delight

8 the name of products which is from one particular company; the trade mark of one particular company

10 a tune; a sequence of notes

12 dreadful; frightful

13 an animal, especially a four-footed one

14 an unsuccessful thing

15 the joint where the arm bends

DOWN

1 a person who lives by begging

2 the measurement or extent of something from side to side; the lesser or least of two or more dimensions of a body

4 a maker or a creator of a film, play, or TV program

5 the act or process of collecting

6 luggage

7 a textile made from a thread produced by silkworms

9 a kind of gentle animal whose neck is very long

11 a measured amount of a medicine given or to be taken at one time

◆上面的遊戲會用到的單字都在這裡！真的看不懂提示就來偷瞄一下吧！

WORD BANK: Baggage, beast, beggar, brand, charm, collection, cupboard, dose, elbow, failure, fearful, giraffe, melody, producer, silk, width.

163

答案就在後面

◆填字遊戲解答在這裡！

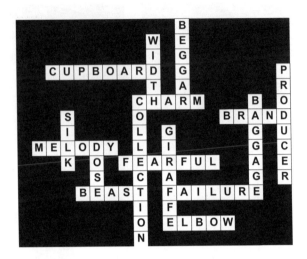

◆單字還記不熟嗎？快來做複習！

baggage [ˋbægɪdʒ] 行李 luggage	**elbow** [ˋɛͺˏbo] 手肘 the joint where the arm bends
beast [bist] 野獸 an animal, especially a four-footed one	**failure** [ˋfeljɚ] 失敗 an unsuccessful thing
beggar [ˋbɛgɚ] 乞丐 a person who lives by begging	**fearful** [ˋfɪrfəl] 可怕的、嚇人的 dreadful; frightful
brand [brænd] 品牌 the name of products which is from one particular company; the trade mark of one particular company	**giraffe** [dʒəˋræf] 長頸鹿 a kind of gentle animal whose neck is very long
charm [tʃɑrm] 魅力 the power or ability to please, attract or delight	**melody** [ˋmɛlədɪ] 旋律 a tune; a sequence of notes
collection [kəˋlɛkʃən] 聚集、收集 the act or process of collecting	**producer** [prəˋdjusɚ] 製造者、製作人、生產者 a maker or a creator of a film, play, or TV program
cupboard [ˋkʌbəd] 食櫥、餐具廚 a piece of furniture with doors, or a set of shelves with doors, where clothes, plates, food, etc., can be stored	**silk** [sɪlk] 絲、綢 a textile made from a thread produced by silkworms
dose [dos] 服藥 a measured amount of a medicine given or to be taken at one time	**width** [wɪdθ] 寬、廣 the measurement or extent of something from side to side; the lesser or least of two or more dimensions of a body

11

◉ 捷徑文化版權所有

◆用英文解釋猜猜英文單字

ACROSS

3 a form of a business or club consisting of a group of people
5 to excite the admiration, interest, or feelings of
7 to tap someone on the shoulder
10 the action of separating something into two or more parts
11 a small soft fleshy red, yellow, or black round fruit with one big seed in the middle
13 cows and bulls especially kept on farm for meat or milk
14 a letter that is delivered by a mailman; to mail
15 a feeling of satisfiction when you have done something well

DOWN

1 to be brave enough or rude enough to do something
2 usually metal rings connected to or fitted into one another, used for fastening, supporting, decorating
4 covering thoroughly; from the beginning to the end
5 anyway
6 having all one's senses working and able to understand what is happening
8 the action of adding one thing to the other
9 the holder of a company
12 considering as true

◆上面的遊戲會用到的單字都在這裡！真的看不懂提示就來偷瞄一下吧！

WORD BANK: Addition, anyhow, attract, boss, cattle, chain, cherry, conscious, dare, division, organization, pat, post, pride, regard, throughout.

答案就在後面

Level-4

◆單字還記不熟嗎？快來做複習！

addition [ə`dɪʃən] 加、加法 the action of adding one thing to the other	**dare** [dɛr] 敢、挑戰 to be brave enough or rude enough to do something
anyhow [`ɛnɪˌhau] 隨便、無論如何 anyway	**division** [də`vɪʒən] 分割、除去 the action of separating something into two or more parts
attract [ə`trækt] 吸引 to excite the admiration, interest, or feelings of	**organization** [ˌɔrgənə`zeʃən] 組織、機構 a form of a business or club consisting of a group of people
boss [bɔs] 老闆、主人 the holder of a company	**pat** [pæt] 輕拍 to tap someone on the shoulder
cattle [`kætl̩] 小牛 cows and bulls especially kept on farm for meat or milk	**post** [post] 郵寄、公佈 a letter that is delivered by a mailman; to mail
chain [tʃen] 鏈、一系列、連續 usually metal rings connected to or fitted into one another, used for fastening, supporting, decorating	**pride** [praɪd] 自豪、得意 a feeling of satisfaction when you have done something well
cherry [`tʃɛrɪ] 櫻桃、櫻木 a small soft fleshy red, yellow, or black round fruit with one big seed in the middle	**regard** [rɪ`gɑrd] 注視、認為 considering as true
conscious [`kɑnʃəs] 意識到的、有知覺的 having all one's senses working and able to understand what is happening	**throughout** [θru`aut] 徹頭徹尾 covering thoroughly; from the beginning to the end

12

◉ 捷徑文化版權所有

◆用英文解釋猜猜英文單字

ACROSS

3 a dark-red hard block, usually used as construction materials
4 the works one must do; a mission
5 of, belonging to, or consisting of the ordinary population of citizens
7 to feel surprized or amazed by someting
10 to form a firm intention or decision
11 weak and about to lose consciousness
13 spectators or listeners at an event
14 a person who makes plans or patterns, especially professionally

DOWN

1 a statement or account that describes
2 something which can fly in the sky; the plane which can take people to other places in the sky
3 the statement of bloodying
6 the act of taking or giving something to someone, or the things taken or given
8 to work in a particular way
9 to push down with stress
12 any object used for attack or defense

◆上面的遊戲會用到的單字都在這裡！真的看不懂提示就來偷瞄一下吧！

WORD BANK: Aircraft, audience, bloody, brick, civil, delivery, description, designer, determine, faint, operate, press, task, weapon, wonder.

167

答案就在後面

Level-4

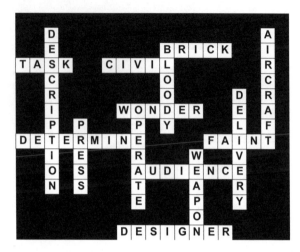

◆單字還記不熟嗎？快來做複習！

aircraft [`ɛr͵kræft] 飛機、飛行器 something which can fly in the sky; the plane which can take people to other places in the sky	**designer** [dɪ`zaɪnɚ] 設計師 a person who makes plans or patterns, especially professionally
audience [`ɔdɪəns] 聽眾、觀眾 spectators or listeners at an event	**determine** [dɪ`tɝmɪn] 決定 to form a firm intention or decision
bloody [`blʌdɪ] 流血的、血淋淋的 the statement of bloodying	**faint** [fent] 昏厥 weak and about to lose consciousness
brick [brɪk] 轉頭、磚塊 a dark-red hard block, usually used as construction materials	**hum** [hʌm] 作嗡嗡聲 make a low, steady continuous sound like that of a bee; the sound of hum
civil [`sɪvl̩] 國家的、公民的 of, belonging to , or consisting of the ordinary population of citizens	**operate** [`ɑpə͵ret] 運轉、操作 to work in a particular way
weapon [`wɛpən] 武器、兵器 any object used for attack or defense	**press** [prɛs] 壓下、強迫 to push down with stress
delivery [dɪ`lɪvərɪ] 傳送、傳遞 the act of taking or giving something to someone, or the things taken or given	**task** [tæsk] 任務 the works one must do; a mission
description [dɪ`skrɪpʃən] 敘述、說明 a statement or account that describes	**wonder** [`wʌndɚ] 對……感到驚奇 to feel surprised or amazed by something

13

◉ 捷徑文化版權所有

◆用英文解釋猜猜英文單字

ACROSS

2 lots of rock; something that is not steal but very hard
3 the science of numbers
6 remove
9 to speack very softly and lightly
10 marked by strong interest or impatient desire
11 the hard outer covering of something, especially nuts, eggs and some animals
14 a public show of objects
15 an exact statement of the meaning, nature, or limits of something, especially of a word of phrase

DOWN

1 any of the seven main large masses of land on the Earth
3 the act of arriving
4 a number of related events happening in a regularly repeated order
5 all the people working on a ship, plane, spacecraft
7 the quality of being excellent
8 a manner of treating someone or something
12 a piece of land used for growing crops or keeping animals; a piece of ground for playing sports or holding contests
13 to heat the liquid so that it's hot enough to turn to gas; to cook something with hot liquid

◆上面的遊戲會用到的單字都在這裡！真的看不懂提示就來偷瞄一下吧！

WORD BANK: Arithmetic, arrival, boil, continent, crew, cycle, definition, eager, erase, excellence, exhibition, field, rocky, shell, treatment, whisper.

169

答案就在後面

◆填字遊戲解答在這裡！

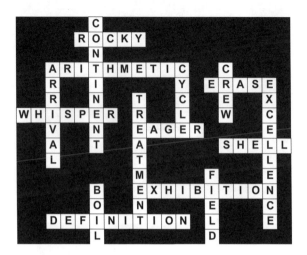

◆單字還記不熟嗎？快來做複習！

arithmetic [ə`rɪθmə͵tɪk] 算術的 the science of numbers	**erase** [ɪ`res] 擦掉、抹去 remove
arrival [ə`raɪvl] 到達 the act of arriving	**excellence** [`ɛksləns] 優點、傑出 the quality of being excellent
boil [bɔɪl] 沸騰、使發怒 to heat the liquid so that it's hot enough to turn to gas; to cook something with hot liquid	**exhibition** [͵ɛksə`bɪʃən] 展覽 a public show of objects
continent [`kɑntənənt] 大陸、陸地 any of the seven main large masses of land on the Earth	**field** [fild] 田野、領域 a piece of land used for growing crops or keeping animals; a piece of ground for playing sports or holding contests
crew [kru] 夥伴、全體船員、機組人員 all the people working on a ship, plane, spacecraft	**rocky** [`rɑkɪ] 岩石的、搖擺的 lots of rock; something that is not steal but very hard
cycle [`saɪkl] 循環 a number of related events happening in a regularly repeated order	**shell** [ʃɛl] 貝殼 the hard outer covering of something, especially nuts, eggs and some animals
definition [͵dɛfə`nɪʃən] 定義 an exact statement of the meaning, nature, or limits of something, especially of a word of phrase	**treatment** [tritmənt] 對待、處理 a manner of treating someone or something
eager [`igɚ] 渴望的 marked by strong interest or impatient desire	**whisper** [`hwɪspɚ] 耳語 to speack very softly and lightly

14

◉ 捷徑文化版權所有

◆用英文解釋猜猜英文單字

ACROSS

2 a living being of any kind, but not a plant

4 someone whose job is to grow and take care of plants in a garden

7 the measurement of how deep the distance is

8 be busy in doing something; in a state of action

9 to take by force

11 a person who is very much liked or loved

12 a ray shinning from something

13 a broad street in a town, sometimes having trees on each side

14 a person who builds and repairs wooden things

DOWN

1 any of the many parts of the covering which grows on a bird's body

2 to become crisp, especially by cooking or heating

3 (especially of a machine) able to work or move by itself without operation by a person

5 to talk in a friendly informal manner

6 a narrow street

9 a system of buying goods or services and paying for them later

10 equality in amount, weight, value or importance, as between two things or the parts of a thing

◆上面的遊戲會用到的單字都在這裡！真的看不懂提示就來偷瞄一下吧！

WORD BANK: Active, alley, automatic, avenue, balance, beam, creature, capture, carpenter, chat, credit, crisp, darling, depth, feather, gardener.

◆填字遊戲解答在這裡！

◆單字還記不熟嗎？快來做複習！

active [ˋæktɪv] 活躍的 be busy in doing something; in a state of action	**carpenter** [ˋkɑrpəntə] 木匠 a person who builds and repairs wooden things
alley [ˋælɪ] 巷、小徑 a narrow street	**chat** [tʃæt] 聊天、閒談 to talk in a friendly informal manner
automatic [ͺͻtəˋmætɪk] 自動的 (especially of a machine) able to work or move by itself without operation by a person	**credit** [ˋkrɛdɪt] 信託、信賴 a system of buying goods or services and paying for them later
avenue [ˋævəͺnju] 大道、大街 a broad street in a town, sometimes having trees on each side	**crisp** [krɪsp] 脆的、清楚的 to become crisp, especially by cooking or heating
balance [ˋbæləns] 使平衡、權衡 equality in amount, weight, value or importance, as between two things or the parts of a thing	**darling** [ˋdɑrlɪŋ] 親愛的人 a person who is very much liked or loved
beam [bin] 放射、發光 a ray shinning from something	**depth** [dɛpθ] 深度、深淵 the measurement of how deep the distance is
creature [ˋkritʃə] 生物、動物 a living being of any kind, but not a plant	**feather** [ˋfɛðə] 羽毛 any of the many parts of the covering which grows on a bird's body
capture [ˋkæptʃə] 攝獲、戰利品 to take by force	**gardener** [ˋgɑrdənə] 園丁、花匠 someone whose job is to grow and take care of plants in a garden

15

◉ 捷徑文化版權所有

◆用英文解釋猜猜英文單字

ACROSS

4 a small area that is connected to a building's second or above floors
6 the enlargement or the development
9 yummy; delicious
10 to present or to exist
12 a small bean used as a food for people and animals
13 a piece of writing with one or several paragraphs which are about a particular subject or issue
14 the sound made by a police car
15 belonging to two or more people

DOWN

1 a nut that grows in pairs inside a thin brown shell
2 a journey made for pleasure
3 of an amount or degree that must be taken seriously
5 to join together or to become joined
7 a material made of several threads twisted together
8 a performance given by a number of musicians
11 being a crime
12 a hard, artificial metal produced by a mixture of iron and carbon

◆上面的遊戲會用到的單字都在這裡！真的看不懂提示就來偷瞄一下吧！

WORD BANK: Article, balcony, beep, concert, connect, considerable, criminal, growth, joint, occur, peanut, soybean, steel, string, tasty, tour.

答案就在後面

◆填字遊戲解答在這裡！

```
            P
            E           T
C       B A L C O N Y   O
O       A           U
N       C U         R
S   G R O W T H
I       N       C         S
D       N     O C C U R   T A S T Y
E   S O Y B E A N   R     R
R   T   C         C     I
A   E   A R T I C L E   N
B E E P           R     G
L   L     J O I N T     
E   L             N
                  A
                  L
```

◆單字還記不熟嗎？快來做複習！

article [`ɑrtɪkḷ] 文章、論文 a piece of writing with one or several paragraphs which are about a particular subject or issue	**joint** [dʒɔɪnt] 接合處 belonging to two or more people
balcony [`bælkənɪ] 陽臺 a small area that is connected to a building's second or above floors	**occur** [ə`kɜ] 發生、存在、出現 to present or to exist
beep [bip] 警笛聲、嗶嗶聲 the sound made by a police car	**peanut** [`piˌnʌt] 花生 a nut that grows in pairs inside a thin brown shell
concert [`kɑnsɝt] 音樂會、演奏會 a performance given by a number of musicians	**soybean** [`sɔɪˋbin] 大豆、黃豆 a small bean used as a food for people and animals
connect [kə`nɛkt] 連接、連結 to join together or to become joined	**steel** [stil] 鋼、鋼鐵 a hard, artificial metal produced by a mixture of iron and carbon
considerable [kən`sɪdərəbḷ] 應考慮的、相當多的 of an amount or degree that must be taken seriously	**string** [strɪŋ] 弦、繩子、一串 a material made of several threads twisted together
criminal [`krɪmənḷ] 罪犯 being a crime	**tasty** [`testɪ] 好吃的 yummy; delicious
growth [groθ] 成長、發育 the enlargement or the development	**tour** [tʊr] 遊覽 a journey made for pleasure

16

◉ 捷徑文化版權所有

◆用英文解釋猜猜英文單字

ACROSS

4 to be accustomed to doing something or a surrounding
6 the order or plans of everything and its details
8 the hair which grows on the bodies of sheep
9 to join together; unite
10 to move steadily and continuously in a current or stream
12 a performance by a travelling group of people and animals who entertain the public with acts of skill and daring
14 at any time
15 to slow down or stop the car suddenly

DOWN

1 a shelter that is made of stones
2 the writer of a book
3 a sweet drink made from lemon juice and water
5 the most powerful evil spirit
6 even if; however
7 an act of placing money in a bank
11 a gentle wind
13 relating to a king, queen or their family

◆上面的遊戲會用到的單字都在這裡！真的看不懂提示就來偷瞄一下吧！

WORD BANK: Although, arrangement, author, brake, breeze, cave, circus, combine, deposit, devil, flow, lemonade, royal, used, whenever, wool.

答案就在後面

◆填字遊戲解答在這裡！

◆單字還記不熟嗎？快來做複習！

although [ɔl`ðo]	**deposit** [dɪ`pɑzɪt]
雖然、縱然 even if; however	存入、放入 an act of placing money in a bank
arrangement [ə`rendʒmənt] 佈置、準備 the order or plans of everything and its details	**devil** [`dɛvl̩] 魔鬼、惡魔 the most powerful evil spirit
author [`ɔθɚ] 作家、作者 the writer of a book	**flow** [flo] 流動 to move steadily and continuously in a current or stream
brake [brek] 煞車 to slow down or stop the car suddenly	**lemonade** [ˌlɛmən`ed] 檸檬水 a sweet drink made from lemon juice and water
breeze [briz] 微風 a gentle wind	**royal** [`rɔɪəl] 皇家的 relating to a king, queen or their family
cave [kev] 洞穴 a shelter that is made of stones	**used** [just] 習慣的 be accustomed to doing something or a surrounding
circus [`sɝkəs] 馬戲團 a performance by a traveling group of people and animals who entertain the public with acts of skill and daring	**whenever** [hwɛn`ɛvɚ] 無論何時 at any time
combine [kəm`baɪn] 聯合、結合 to join together; unite	**wool** [wʊl] 羊毛 the hair which grows on the bodies of sheep

17

◉ 捷徑文化版權所有

◆用英文解釋猜猜英文單字

ACROSS

2 the very large brown hard-shelled nut-like fruit of a tall tropical tree, with white flesh and a hollow center filled with juice

3 to startle someone usually with an unpleasant event

5 separated by a distance

7 to be able to buy or pay for

9 level and smooth, with no curved, high, or hollow parts

10 that happened or began only a short time ago

11 to act in a certain manner to control your actions

12 to make deaf, especially for a short time

13 to throw suddenly; to settle a tent; the state of throwing

DOWN

1 a door, gate

2 male chicken; rooster

3 to solve a problem; to put an argument or disagreement to the end

4 a decorative covering for the head, use made of gold and jewels, worn by a king or queen as a sign of royal power

6 fear; terror

7 to join in; to be present

8 below or under

◆上面的遊戲會用到的單字都在這裡！真的看不懂提示就來偷瞄一下吧！

WORD BANK: Afford, apart, attend, behave, beneath, cock, coconut, crown, deafen, fright, entry, flat, pitch, recent, settle, shock.

答案就在後面

◆填字遊戲解答在這裡！

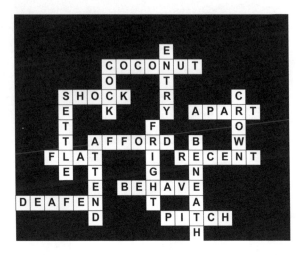

◆單字還記不熟嗎？快來做複習！

afford [əˋford] 供給、能負擔 to be able to buy or pay for	**deafen** [ˋdɛfən] 使耳聾 to make deaf, especially for a short time
apart [əˋpɑrt] 分散地、遠離地 separated by a distance	**fright** [fraɪt] 驚駭、恐怖、驚嚇 fear; terror
attend [əˋtɛnd] 出席、照料 to join in; to be present	**entry** [ˋɛntrɪ] 入口 a door, gate
behave [bɪˋhev] 行動、舉止 to act in a certain manner to control your actions	**flat** [flæt] 平的、公寓 level and smooth, with no curved, high, or hollow parts
beneath [bɪˋniθ] 在……下面 below or under	**pitch** [pɪtʃ] 投擲 to throw suddenly; to settle a tent; the state of throwing
cock [kɑk] 公雞 male chicken; rooster	**recent** [ˋrisn̩t] 最近的 that happened or began only a short time ago
coconut [ˋkokəˏnət] 椰子 the very large brown hard-shelled nut-like fruit of a tall tropical tree, with white flesh and a hollow center filled with juice	**settle** [ˋsɛtl̩] 安排、解決 to solve a problem; to put an argument or disagreement to the end
crown [kraʊn] 王冠 a decorative covering for the head, use made of gold and jewels, worn by a king or queen as a sign of royal power	**shock** [ʃɑk] 震撼、震驚 to startle someone usually with an unpleasant event

18

◉ 捷徑文化版權所有

◆用英文解釋猜猜英文單字

ACROSS

2 can be counted
3 having knowledge or understanding
5 rather cold
6 to move slowly with the body close to the ground
8 conventional; customary
9 one thousand million
12 a person or animal that has won a competition of skill, strength
13 a vehicle with two or four wheels used for carrying things
14 a legal relationship in which two people have pledged to live as husband and wife

DOWN

1 a part of the human body which contains the stomach, intestines
2 a country or area under the political control of a distant country
4 the state of existing
7 a particular area
9 a number of things fastened, held, or growing together at one point
10 the inside part of the hand
11 a piece of thin metal thread

◆上面的遊戲會用到的單字都在這裡！真的看不懂提示就來偷瞄一下吧！

WORD BANK: Aware, billion, belly, bunch, cart, champion, chilly, colony, countable, crawl, existence, marriage, palm, region, traditional wire.

Level-4

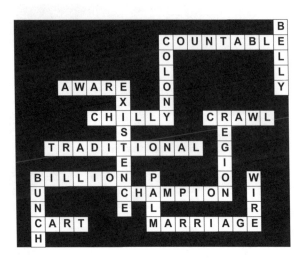

◆單字還記不熟嗎？快來做複習！

aware [əˈwɛr] 注意到的、覺察的 having knowledge or understanding	**countable** [ˈkaʊntəbl̩] 可數的 can be counted
billion [ˈbɪljən] 十億、一兆 one thousand million	**crawl** [krɔl] 爬 to move slowly with the body close to the ground
belly [ˈbɛlɪ] 腹、胃 a part of the human body which contains the stomach, intestines	**existence** [ɪgˈzɪstəns] 存在 the state of existing
bunch [bʌntʃ] 束、串、捆 a number of things fastened, held, or growing together at one point	**marriage** [ˈmærɪdʒ] 婚姻 a legal relationship in which two people have pledged to live as husband and wife
cart [kɑrt] 手拉車 a vehicle with two or four wheels used for carrying things	**palm** [pɑm] 手掌 the inside part of the hand
champion [ˈtʃæmpɪən] 冠軍 a person or animal that has won a competition of skill, strength	**region** [ˈridʒən] 區域 a particular area
chilly [ˈtʃɪlɪ] 寒冷的 rather cold	**traditional** [trəˈdɪʃənl̩] 傳統的 conventional; customary
colony [ˈkɑlənɪ] 殖民者 a country or area under the political control of a distant country	**wire** [waɪr] 金屬絲、電線 a piece of thin metal thread

19

◉ 捷徑文化版權所有

◆用英文解釋猜猜英文單字

ACROSS

4 relating to an authority of responsibilities; a person who is having official duties
5 anything used as a lure
7 an unexpected and dangerous happening which must be dealt with at once
11 dry powder made of extremely small grains of waste matter
12 money which is earned by working
13 far on in development
15 the quality of being able to do something
16 to divide into parts; to distinquish from; to break up; individual

DOWN

1 the fight between two countries in order to strive land, energy, etc.
2 a narrow boat with pointed ends and move with one or more paddles
3 a place on a farm where milk is kept and butter and cheese are made
6 a black and white flightless sea bird with wings modified as flippers to help it swim
8 happy and lively
9 quick-moving
10 a device with two sharp blades used for cutting papper, clothes, etc.
14 throw with force

◆上面的遊戲會用到的單字都在這裡！真的看不懂提示就來偷瞄一下吧！

WORD BANK: Ability, advanced, bait, battle, canoe, cast, cheerful, dairy, dust, earnings, emergency, official, penguin, rapid, scissors, separate.

答案就在後面

◆填字遊戲解答在這裡！

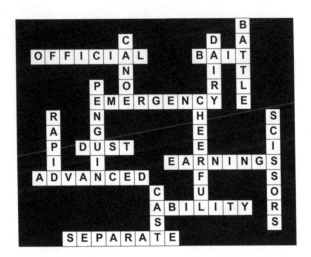

◆單字還記不熟嗎？快來做複習！

ability [ə`bɪlətɪ] 能力 the quality of being able to do something	**dust** [dʌst] 灰塵、灰 dry powder made of extremely small grains of waste matter
advanced [əd`vænst] 在前面的、先進的 far on in development	**earnings** [`ɜnɪŋz] 收入 money which is earned by working
bait [bet] 誘惑、餌 anything used as a lure	**emergency** [ɪ`mɜdʒənsɪ] 緊急情況 an unexpected and dangerous happening which must be dealt with at once
battle [`bætl] 戰役 the fight between two countries in order to strive land, energy, etc.	**official** [ə`fɪʃəl] 官員的; 公務上的 relating to an authority of responsibilities; a person who is having official duties
cast [kæst] 投、演員班底、石膏 throw with force	**penguin** [`pɛngwɪn] 企鵝 a black and white flightless sea bird with wings modified as flippers to help it swim
canoe [kə`nu] 獨木舟 a narrow boat with pointed ends and move with one or more paddles	**rapid** [`ræpɪd] 迅速的 quick-moving
cheerful [`tʃɪrfəl] 愉快的、興高采烈的 happy and lively	**scissors** [`sɪzəz] 剪刀 a device with two sharp blades used for cutting papper, clothes, etc.
dairy [`dɛrɪ] 酪農的 a place on a farm where milk is kept and butter and cheese are made	**separate** [`sɛpərɪt] 分開 to divide into parts; to distinguish from; to break up; individual

20

◉ 捷徑文化版權所有

◆用英文解釋猜猜英文單字

ACROSS

3 the act of choosing; the thing or person that's selected
6 a specialist or a professional
7 government by the people, or by elected representatives of the people
8 of the usual or ordinary kind
11 being simple or easy to understand
13 closely to standard
15 the state of things as they are; the true situation
16 plus, usually used when one has something more to add for what just mentioned

DOWN

1 difficult to understand, explain, or deal with
2 to have a favorable opinion
4 giving pleasure
5 any of various kinds of small plastic or metal objects used for holding things tightly together or in place
9 to help or support
10 the one who does something at first time; the green hands
12 a small beetle with black spots on its brightly colored round body
14 to flow off gradually or completely

◆上面的遊戲會用到的單字都在這裡！真的看不懂提示就來偷瞄一下吧！

WORD BANK: Accurate, approve, assist, average, beginner, besides, brief, clip, complex, democracy, drain, enjoyable, expert, ladybug, reality, selection.

答案就在後面

Level-4

◆填字遊戲解答在這裡！

A crossword puzzle grid with the following words: SELECTION, COMPLEX, EXPERT, ENJOYABLE, CLIP, APPROVE, DEMOCRACY, AVERAGE, ASSIST, BRIEF, BEGINNER, ACCURATE, LADYBUG, DRAIN, REALITY, BESIDES

◆單字還記不熟嗎？快來做複習！

accurate [ˈækjərɪt] 正確的、準確的 closely to standard	**complex** [ˈkɑmplɛks] 複合物、綜合設施 difficult to understand, explain, or deal with
approve [əˈpruv] 批准、認可 to have a favorable opinion	**democracy** [dəˈmɑkrəsɪ] 民主制度 government by the people, or by elected representatives of the people
assist [əˈsɪst] 說明、援助 to help or support	**drain** [dren] 排出、流出、喝乾 to flow off gradually or completely
average [ˈævərɪdʒ] 平均數 of the usual or ordinary kind	**enjoyable** [ɪnˈdʒɔɪəbl̩] 愉快的 giving pleasure
beginner [bɪˈgɪnɚ] 初學者 the one who does something at first time; the green hands	**expert** [ˈɛkspɚt] 專家 a specialist or a professional
besides [bɪˈsaɪdz] 並且 plus, usually used when one has something more to add for what just mentioned	**ladybug** [ˈledɪˌbʌg] 瓢蟲 a small beetle with black spots on its brightly colored round body
brief [brif] 摘要、短文 being simple or easy to understand	**reality** [rɪˈælətɪ] 真實 the state of things as they are; the true situation
clip [klɪp] 夾子、紙夾、修剪 any of various kinds of small plastic or metal objects used for holding things tightly together or in place	**selection** [səˈlɛkʃən] 選擇、選定 the act of choosing; the thing or person that's selected

21

◉ 捷徑文化版權所有

◆用英文解釋猜猜英文單字

ACROSS

6 to make an effort at
8 actions that are brave
9 to set in a particular place
11 to try to win something in competition with someone else
13 to make a round hole or passage
14 to move slowly, quietly, and carefully
15 to make a noise like the sound of something being crushed
16 a tall solid upright stone post used in a building as a support or decoration or standing alone as a monument

DOWN

1 the person who is famous for his poem and writing poems as his career
2 later; after that
3 a strip of cloth used to bind or cover an injured part
4 a substance that can be used to produce others
5 to put (a dead body) into a grave
7 on the face of something
10 a dull, continuous pain
12 greatest possible

◆上面的遊戲會用到的單字都在這裡！真的看不懂提示就來偷瞄一下吧！

WORD BANK: Ache, afterward, attempt, bandage, bore, bravery, bury, column, compete, creep, crunchy, extreme, locate, material, poet, surface.

185

答案就在後面

Level-4

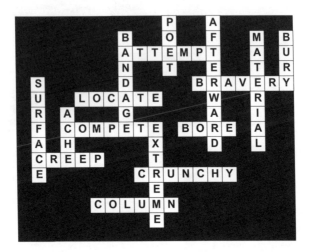

◆單字還記不熟嗎？快來做複習！

ache [ek] 疼痛 a dull, continuous pain	**compete** [kəm`pit] 競爭、對抗、比賽 to try to win something in competition with someone else
afterward [`æftəwəd(z)] 以後 later; after that	**creep** [krip] 爬 to move slowly, quietly, and carefully
attempt [ə`tɛmpt] 嘗試、企圖 to make an effort at	**crunchy** [`krʌntʃɪ] 鬆脆的、易裂的 to make a noise like the sound of something being crushed
bandage [`bændɪdʒ] 繃帶 a strip of cloth used to bind or cover an injured part	**extreme** [ɪk`strim] 極度的 greatest possible
bore [bor] 鑽孔 to make a round hole or passage	**locate** [lo`ket] 設置、居住 to set in a particular place
bravery [`brevərɪ] 大膽、勇敢 actions that are brave	**material** [mə`tɪrɪəl] 物質 a substance that can be used to produce others
bury [`bɛrɪ] 埋 to put (a dead body) into a grave	**poet** [`poɪt] 詩人 the person who is famous for his poem and writing poems as his career
column [`kɑləm] 圓柱、專欄、欄 a tall solid upright stone post used in a building as a support or decoration or standing alone as a monument	**surface** [`sɝfɪs] 表面 on the face of something

22

◉ 捷徑文化版權所有

◆用英文解釋猜猜英文單字

ACROSS

1 the fleshy part of the face below the eye, especially in humans

4 a building where people are kept as a punishment for a crime they have commited

7 a small bed for a baby, especially one made so that it can be moved gently from side to side

10 a kind of tall, slim plants which is hollowed

11 to make known publicly

12 the characteristic of something; the standard of something when compared to other thins similar to it

14 the state of being related with someone or something

DOWN

1 to have a sudden, violent, and noisy accident

2 the scenery or space behind the main objects or people in a view, a picture, or a photograph

3 someone who appears in fire place and try any way to put it out

5 a significant other or spouse; come together to breed offspring

6 a manner

7 a person who gets help and advice from a professional person

8 toward the direction that is opposite to yours

9 the argument between people or organizations

13 to take into one's own family by legal process and raise as one's own

◆上面的遊戲會用到的單字都在這裡！真的看不懂提示就來偷瞄一下吧！

WORD BANK: Adopt, announce, background, backwards, bamboo, cheek, client, conflict, cradle, crash, fireman, mate, means, prison, quality, relationship.

答案就在後面

◆填字遊戲解答在這裡！

```
      C H E E K           B
  F   R                   A
      A                   C
P R I S O N       M   M   K
  E   H       C R A D L E G       B
  M   C       L   T   A   R       A
B A M B O O   I   E   A N N O U N C E
  N   N       E       S   U       K
      F       N       A   N       W
  Q U A L I T Y       A   D       A
        I             D           R
        C             O           D
  R E L A T I O N S H I P         S
                      T
```

◆單字還記不熟嗎？快來做複習！

adopt [ə'dɑpt] 收養、採取 to take into one's own family by legal process and raise as one's own	**cradle** ['kredl] 搖籃 a small bed for a baby, especially one made so that it can be moved gently from side to side
announce [ə'naʊs] 宣佈、宣告 to make known publicly	**crash** [kræʃ] 摔下、撞毀 to have a sudden, violent, and noisy accident
background ['bæk‚graʊnd] 背景 the scenery or space behind the main objects or people in a view, a picture, or a photograph	**fireman** ['faɪrmən] 消防員 someone who appears in fire place and try any way to put it out
backwards ['bækwədz] 向後 toward the direction that is opposite to yours	**mate** [met] 配對、同伴、配偶 a significant other or spouse; come together to breed offspring
bamboo [bæm'bu] 竹子 a kind of tall, slim plants which is hollowed	**means** [minz] 方法 a manner
cheek [tʃik] 臉頰 the fleshy part of the face below the eye, especially in humans	**quality** ['kwɑlətɪ] 品質 the characteristic of something; the standard of something when compared to other thins similar to it
client ['klaɪənt] 委託人、客戶 a person who gets help and advice from a professional person	**prison** ['prɪzn̩] 監獄 a building where people are kept as a punishment for a crime they have commited
conflict ['kɑnflɪkt] 衝突 the argument between people or organizations	**relationship** [rɪ'leʃənˏʃɪp] 關係 the state of being related with someone or something

23

◉ 捷徑文化版權所有

◆用英文解釋猜猜英文單字

ACROSS

3 a round fruit with yellow or green skin, sweet juicy flesh and lots of seeds
4 a kind of weapons that is made to explode; to attack a place with materials that can explode
5 an official agreement that ends an argument between two people or groups
7 the science and art of farming
11 not serious; like to play
12 working well, quickly, and without waste
13 to trouble someone when he is working or studying
14 completely true, following all guidelines or precise
15 full of juice

DOWN

1 something that helps to find an answer to a question, difficulty, or mystery
2 to get someone dressed; to put on clothes
3 to increase largely in number
6 either of the two parts of a woman's body that produce milk
8 the amount of vehicles moving along a street
9 to look after a baby
10 to keep; to go on one statement

◆上面的遊戲會用到的單字都在這裡！真的看不懂提示就來偷瞄一下吧！

WORD BANK: Agriculture, baby-sit, bomb, bother, breast, clothe, clue, efficient, exact, juicy, maintain, melon, multiply, playful, settlement, traffic.

答案就在後面

◆填字遊戲解答在這裡！

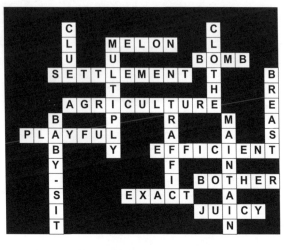

◆單字還記不熟嗎？快來做複習！

agriculture [ˈægrɪˌkʌltʃɚ] 農業、農藝、農學 the science and art of farming	**exact** [ɪgˈzækt] 正確的、確切的 completely true, following all guidelines or precise
baby-sit [ˈbebɪˌsɪt] 照顧嬰孩 to look after a baby	**juicy** [ˈdʒusɪ] 多汁的 full of juice
bomb [bɑm] 炸彈 a kind of weapons that is made to explode; to attack a place with materials that can explode	**maintain** [menˈten] 維持 to keep; to go on one statement
bother [ˈbɑðɚ] 打擾 to trouble someone when he is working or studying	**melon** [ˈmɛlən] 瓜、甜瓜 a round fruit with yellow or green skin, sweet juicy flesh and lots of seeds
breast [brɛst] 胸膛、胸部 either of the two parts of a woman's body that produce milk	**multiply** [ˈmʌltəplaɪ] 增加、繁殖、相乘 to increase largely in number
clothe [kloð] 穿衣、給……穿衣 to get someone dressed; to put on clothes	**playful** [ˈplefəl] 愛玩的 not serious; like to play
clue [klu] 線索 something that helps to find an answer to a question, difficulty, or mystery	**settlement** [ˈsɛtl̩mənt] 解決、安排 an official agreement that ends an argument between two people or groups
efficient [ɪˈfɪʃənt] 有效率的 working well, quickly, and without waste	**traffic** [ˈtræfɪk] 交通 the amount of vehicles moving along a street

24

◉ 捷徑文化版權所有

◆用英文解釋猜猜英文單字

ACROSS

4 the amount or number of something, especially that can be measured or is fixed

5 formal indication of a choice between two or more candidates or courses of action; to give a vote

6 air taken into and breathed out of the lungs

9 the act of exchanging

12 a kind of mineral that is black and hard, used to produce heat

14 a sound sent back or repeated from a surface

15 to use practically; to make a request for something or some place

16 to schedule everything in order

DOWN

1 any of the main divisions of a book or long article, usually having a number or title

2 to take a number or an amount from a larger number ot amount

3 a hollow ball of air or gas in a liquid

7 very bad or unpleasant

8 someone who officially owns something

10 a town which is the center of government of a country or other political unit

11 the mark used in writing and printing for showing a short pause

13 a part of the body which has particular functions

◆上面的遊戲會用到的單字都在這裡！真的看不懂提示就來偷瞄一下吧！

WORD BANK: Apply, arrange, awful, breath, bubble, capital, chapter, coal, comma, echo, exchange, holder, organ, quantity, subtract, vote.

答案就在後面

Level-4

◆填字遊戲解答在這裡！

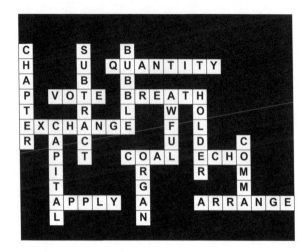

◆單字還記不熟嗎？快來做複習！

apply [ə`plaɪ] 請求、應用、塗敷 to use practically; to make a request for something or some place	**comma** [`kɑmə] 逗號 the mark used in writing and printing for showing a short pause
arrange [ə`rendʒ] 安排、籌備 to schedule everything in order	**echo** [`ɛko] 回音 a sound sent back or repeated from a surface
awful [`ɔful] 可怕的、嚇人的 very bad or unpleasant	**exchange** [ɪks`tʃendʒ] 交換 the act of exchanging
breath [brɛθ] 呼吸、氣息 air taken into and breathed out of the lungs	**holder** [`holdɚ] 持有者、所有人 someone who officially owns something
bubble [`bʌbl̩] 泡沫、氣泡 a hollow ball of air or gas in a liquid	**organ** [`ɔrgən] 器官 a part of the body which has particular functions
capital [`kæpətl̩] 主要的、首都 a town which is the center of government of a country or other political unit	**quantity** [`kwɑntətɪ] 數量 the amount or number of something, especially that can be measured or is fixed
chapter [`tʃæptɚ] 章、章節 any of the main divisions of a book or long article, usually having a number or title	**subtract** [səb`trækt] 扣除、移走 to take a number or an amount from a larger number ot amount
coal [kol] 煤 a kind of mineral that is black and hard, used to produce heat	**vote** [vot] 投票 formal indication of a choice between two or more candidates or courses of action; to give a vote

25

◉ 捷徑文化版權所有

◆用英文解釋猜猜英文單字

ACROSS

1 the seed of some plants which is round-shaped and sometimes can be served as food
6 a small brown insect, the male of which makes loud short noises by rubbing its leathery wings together
7 the next; the coming
10 mateiral wealth or valuable objects
11 to come near
13 to become cold, especially without freezing
14 imaginative and inventive
16 a chance that something may happen

DOWN

2 connected with the environment
3 a person who is employed
4 likely to change
5 a person in a stated type of businessan
8 cookie
9 ahead
12 a plan that is officially executed for the sake of improvement
15 to prepare for printing, broadcasting by deciding what shall be included

◆上面的遊戲會用到的單字都在這裡！真的看不懂提示就來偷瞄一下吧！

WORD BANK: Approach, bean, biscuit, changeable, chill, creative, cricket, dealer, edit, employee, environmental, following, forwards, policy, possibility, riches.

193

答案就在後面

◆填字遊戲解答在這裡！

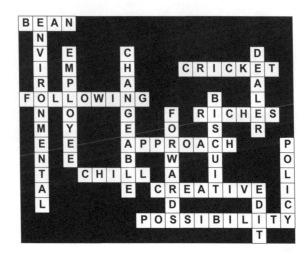

◆單字還記不熟嗎？快來做複習！

approach [əˋprotʃ] 接近 to come near	**edit** [ˋɛdɪt] 編輯、發行 to prepare for printing, broadcasting by deciding what shall be included
bean [bin] 豆子 the seed of some plants which is round-shaped and sometimes can be served as food	**employee** [ˏɛmplɔɪˋi] 職員 a person who is employed
biscuit [ˋbɪskɪt] 餅乾 cookie	**environmental** [ɪnˋvaɪrənmənt!] 環境的 connected with the environment
changeable [ˋtʃendʒəb!] 可變的 likely to change	**following** [ˋfaləwɪŋ] 下一個 the next; the coming
chill [tʃɪl] 使變冷 to become cold, especially without freezing	**forwards** [ˋfɔrwədz] 今後、將來、向前 ahead
creative [krɪˋetɪv] 有創造力的 imaginative and inventive	**policy** [ˋpaləsɪ] 政策 a plan that is officially executed for the sake of improvement
cricket [ˋkrɪkɪt] 蟋蟀 a small brown insect, the male of which makes loud short noises by rubbing its leathery wings together	**possibility** [ˏpasəˋbɪlətɪ] 可能性 a chance that something may happen
dealer [ˋdilə] 商人 a person in a stated type of businessman	**riches** [ˋrɪtʃɪz] 財產 material wealth or valuable objects

26

◉ 捷徑文化版權所有

◆用英文解釋猜猜英文單字

ACROSS

3 a flat circular piece of plastic used for storing computer information
5 a diplomat of the highest rank who is the official representative of his country in another country
8 to like one thing better than the other
10 not to like
12 almost not
13 the money which needs to be paid when you expend on food or merchandise
14 near in a position
16 full of feeling and meaning

DOWN

1 the dividing line between two countries
2 used to express the cost or amount of something for each person
4 in an easy way
6 the space between two lines or surfaces that meet or cross each other, measured in degrees that represent the amount of a circle that can fir into that space
7 thinking that something is worth believing
9 the measurement of something from the beginning to the end
11 to blow up
15 without clothes or covering

◆上面的遊戲會用到的單字都在這裡！真的看不懂提示就來偷瞄一下吧！

WORD BANK: Ambassador, angle, bare, barely, believable, bill, border, disk, dislike, explode, expressive, length, nearby, per, prefer, simply.

答案就在後面

◆填字遊戲解答在這裡！

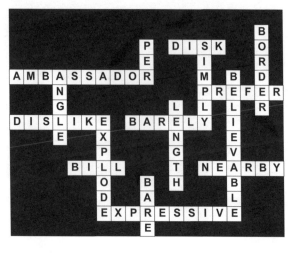

◆單字還記不熟嗎？快來做複習！

ambassador [æmˋbæsədɚ] 大使 a diplomat of the highest rank who is the official representative of his country in another country	**dislike** [dɪsˋlaɪk] 不喜歡 not to like
angle [ˋæŋg!] 角度、立場 the space between two lines or surfaces that meet or cross each other	**explode** [ɪkˋsplod] 爆炸 to blow up
bare [bɛr] 暴露的、僅有的 without clothes or covering	**expressive** [ɪkˋsprɛsɪv] 表達的 full of feeling and meaning
barely [ˋbɛrlɪ] 簡直沒有、幾乎不能 almost not	**length** [lɛŋθ] 長度 the measurement of something from the beginning to the end
believable [bɪˋlivəb!] 可信任的 thinking that something is worth believing	**nearby** [ˋnɪrˏbaɪ] 不遠地 near in a position
bill [bɪl] 帳單 the money which needs to be paid when you expend on food or merchandise	**per** [pɚ] 每、經由 used to express the cost or amount of something for each person
border [ˋbɔrdɚ] 邊界、國界 the dividing line between two countries	**prefer** [prɪˋfɝ] 偏愛、較喜歡 to like one thing better than the other
disk [dɪsk] 唱片、碟片、圓盤狀的東西 a flat circular piece of plastic used for storing computer information	**simply** [ˋsɪmplɪ] 簡單地、樸實地 in an easy way

27

◉ 捷徑文化版權所有

◆用英文解釋猜猜英文單字

ACROSS

3 to do business; the activity of buying and selling, or exchanging

5 refering that something is used by someone

7 the need for something; to ask for something

8 a building or part of a hospital where usually specialized medical treatment and advice is given to outpatients

9 a period of ten years

13 being successful or having fortune by chance

14 a large cylindrical container with flat, circular ends which is used for storing wine or other liquids

15 dissatisfaction

DOWN

1 the state of being in a particular place

2 to marry

4 a journey, experience that is strange and exciting and often dangerous

6 a small soft fruit with seeds

9 a place where ships are loaded and unloaded, or repaired

10 give a job to

11 to provide something for those who need it; the stocks

12 a small private room

◆上面的遊戲會用到的單字都在這裡！真的看不懂提示就來偷瞄一下吧！

WORD BANK: Adventure, barrel, berry, cabin, clinic, complaint, decade, dock, employ, luck, presence, require, supply, trade, used, wed.

答案就在後面

Level-4

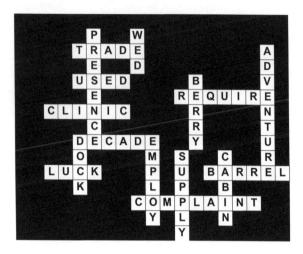

◆單字還記不熟嗎？快來做複習！

adventure [ədˋvɛntʃɚ] 冒險 a journey, experience that is strange and exciting and often dangerous	**employ** [ɪmˋplɔɪ] 從事、雇用 give a job to
barrel [ˋbærəl] 桶、一桶的量 a large cylindrical container with flat, circular ends which is used for storing wine or other liquids	**luck** [lʌk] 幸運 being successful or having fortune by chance
berry [ˋbɛrɪ] 漿果、莓 a small soft fruit with seeds	**presence** [ˋprɛzn̩s] 出席 the state of being in a particular place
cabin [ˋkæbɪn] 小屋、茅屋 a small private room	**require** [rɪˋkwaɪr] 需要 the need for something; to ask for something
clinic [ˋklɪnɪk] 診所 a building or part of a hospital where usually specialized medical treatment and advice is given to outpatients	**supply** [səˋplaɪ] 供給 to provide something for those who need it; the stocks
complaint [kəmˋplent] 抱怨、訴苦 dissatisfaction	**trade** [tred] 交易 to do business; the activity of buying and selling, or exchanging
decade [ˋdɛked] 十年、十個一組 a period of ten years	**used** [juzd] 用過的、二手的 refering that something is used by someone
dock [dɑk] 船塢、碼頭 a place where ships are loaded and unloaded, or repaired	**wed** [wɛd] 嫁、娶、結婚 to marry

28

◉ 捷徑文化版權所有

◆用英文解釋猜猜英文單字

ACROSS

2 having a hard surface or structure
3 a single point or fact about something
6 to become greater in width
9 a person who edits
10 easily seen or understood
11 a place where sells breads, toasts or cakes
12 fixed or unchanging
13 to finish successfully
14 someone or something that is very bright, either in terms of intelligence or because it is shiny

DOWN

1 a kind of brown nuts
3 to avoid something by moving suddenly aside
4 an example; to set an example
5 to die by being under water and unable to breathe
7 an indoor sport in which one roll a heavy ball along a wooden track
8 to make longer or wider
10 strong request for help, support, kindness

◆上面的遊戲會用到的單字都在這裡！真的看不懂提示就來偷瞄一下吧！

WORD BANK: Achieve, almond, apparent, appeal, bakery, bowling, brilliant, constant, detail, dodge, drown, editor, firm, instance, stretch, widen.

答案就在後面

Level-4

◆填字遊戲解答在這裡！

◆單字還記不熟嗎？快來做複習！

achieve [ə`tʃiv] 完成、實現 to finish successfully	**detail** [`ditel] 細節、條款 a single point or fact about something
almond [`amənd] 杏仁、杏樹 a kind of brown nuts	**dodge** [dɑdʒ] 閃躲 to avoid something by moving suddenly aside
apparent [ə`pærənt] 明顯的、外表的 easily seen or understood	**drown** [draʊn] 淹沒、淹死 to die by being under water and unable to breathe
appeal [ə`pil] 引起……的興趣、訴諸 strong request for help, support, kindness	**editor** [`ɛdɪtɚ] 編輯 a person who edits
bakery [`bekərɪ] 麵包店 a place where sells breads, toasts or cakes	**firm** [fɝm] 牢固的、堅定的 having a hard surface or structure
bowling [`bolɪŋ] 保齡球 an indoor sport in which one roll a heavy ball along a wooden track	**instance** [`ɪnstəns] 舉證、例子 an example; to set an example
brilliant [`brɪljənt] 有才氣的、出色的 someone or something that is very bright, either in terms of intelligence or because it is shiny	**stretch** [strɛtʃ] 伸展 to make longer or wider
constant [`kɑnstənt] 不變的、不斷的 fixed or unchanging	**widen** [`waɪdn̩] 使……變寬、增廣 to become greater in width

29

◉ 捷徑文化版權所有

◆用英文解釋猜猜英文單字

ACROSS

2 advantage or profit
5 existing as a real fact
8 to move forward; raise in amount
10 not asleep
11 a reduction made in the cost of buying goods
14 a custom or a convention
15 of or favoring democracy
16 to control the public affairs of a group, a company, or a country

DOWN

1 a person trained in exercises
3 the making of pots, tiles, etc., by shaping pieces of clay and baking them until they are hard
4 no matter what
6 a mixed alcoholic drink
7 a tool with a heavy metal blade on the end of a long handle, used to cut down trees or split logs
9 a schoolchild
12 being like a bone or being very thin
13 the end; finale

◆上面的遊戲會用到的單字都在這裡！真的看不懂提示就來偷瞄一下吧！

WORD BANK: Actual, advance, athlete, awake, axe, benefit, bony, ceramic, cocktail, democratic, discount, ending, govern, pupil, tradition, whatever.

答案就在後面

Level-4

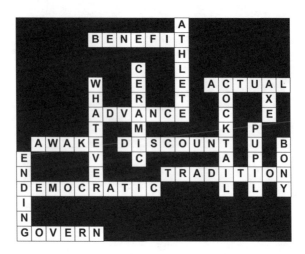

◆單字還記不熟嗎？快來做複習！

actual [`æktʃʊəl] 實際的、真實的 existing as a real fact	**cocktail** [`kɑkˌtel] 雞尾酒 a mixed alcoholic drink
advance [əd`væns] 前進 to move forward; raise in amount	**democratic** [ˌdɛmə`krætɪk] 民主的 of or favoring democracy
athlete [`æθlit] 運動員 a person trained in exercises	**discount** [`dɪskaʊnt] 減價、打折扣 a reduction made in the cost of buying goods
awake [ə`wek] 喚醒 not asleep	**pupil** [`pjupl̩] 學生、學徒 a schoolchild
axe [æks] 劈、砍 a tool with a heavy metal blade on the end of a long handle, used to cut down trees or split logs	**ending** [`ɛndɪŋ] 結局、結束 the end; finale
benefit [`bɛnəfɪt] 獲益 advantage or profit	**govern** [`gʌvɚn] 統治、治理 to control the public affairs of a group, a company, or a country
bony [`bonɪ] 多骨的、骨瘦如柴的 being like a bone or being very thin	**tradition** [trə`dɪʃən] 傳統 a custom or a convention
ceramic [sə`ræmɪk] 陶瓷品 the making of pots, tiles, etc., by shaping pieces of clay and baking them until they are hard	**whatever** [hwɑt`ɛvɚ] 任何 no matter what

Let's talk about fast fashion

Nowadays, fashion retailers like Zara, H&M create "52 micro seasons" each year. In order for the mass public to enjoy latest fashion style presented at Fashion weeks at a rather lower price, the founder of Zara, Amancio Ortega, pioneered the current mode of fast fashion. Zara largely compressed the traditional fashion production cycles. Ortega once proudly said it would only take 15 days for a garment to go from a designer's brain to being sold on the racks.

However, under the fashionable surface, several severe problems have been created by fast fashion. One of the hidden truths is that fast fashion is created to let people feel out of trend after a week. With new goods keep coming out, people buy more and thus create more waste. Low price and constant discounts also imply for exploitation of labor. Worst of all, a few companies use heavy metal contaminated materials to produce garments. It causes environmental damages as well as health issues.

Try to think twice next time when you want to buy fast fashion clothing. Just because it has dominated the fashion industry, it doesn't mean that you need to catch up with it!

來談談快時尚吧！

現今，時尚產業零售商如Zara、H&M把一年劃分成52個季度。為了讓大眾可以用相對低廉的價格享受到時尚周中出現的最新款式，Zara的創辦人阿曼西歐奧蒂嘉成為當今快時尚模式的先驅。Zara很大程度的壓縮了傳統時尚產業的生產週期。奧蒂嘉曾經驕傲的提過，一件衣服從在設計師的腦子裡構想，到最後在貨架上販賣只需要15天。

然而，隱含在光鮮亮麗的時尚表面後，快時尚創造出了一些嚴重的問題。快時尚隱含最大的其一真相便是它的誕生是為了讓人們在一週的時間後就覺得自己脫離潮流，而只要新商品不斷推出，人們就會買得更多、也創造出更多浪費。低廉售價和經常折扣的性質則暗示著快時尚對勞工的剝削。最糟糕的是，有些公司使用被重金屬汙染的原料生產商品，對環境和人體健康造成損害。

下次當你想購買快時尚服飾時，試著三思吧，即使它已經支配了整個時尚產業，並不代表你必須要追趕這一波流行。

Why take a gap year?

After graduating from high school or university, many young people choose to take a short break in life. They take a gap year. What are the potential benefits from doing so?

Gap year often means traveling, volunteering or working aboard. While going on a global adventure, one can immerse in exotic cultures, seize the opportunity to learn new languages and make friends with people from all around the world. Experience things that you never try before can also be a good option. Gap year could be a precious experience of lifetime if used well. For people who hesitate about their career choice or passion for life, gap year can be helpful as well. By taking some time off to examine current life and values, one may eventually develop new life skills or discover hidden passion during gap year.

Finally, for anyone who consider about taking a gap year, here are a few tips. Do plenty of research beforehand and ask people who have done it. Control your budget and take some quality time to make plans. Be open-minded since gap year is all about new experiences. At last, remember to enjoy every moment!

為什麼選擇空檔年？

高中或大學畢業後，許多年輕人會選擇在人生中稍微短暫休息，他們會給自己一個空檔年（gap year）。這樣的潛在益處有什麼呢？

空檔年經常和旅行、當志工和到國外工作劃上等號。到世界各地探險的同時，可以讓自己沉浸在異國文化中、把握機會學習新的語言，並和來自世界各地的人交朋友，體驗從未嘗試過的事也會是一個好選擇。如果好好運用空檔年，這將會是一輩子寶貴的經驗。對於那些對未來職業選擇有疑慮，或找不到自己人生熱情所在的人，空檔年也有所助益。花上一些時間好好審視自己目前的人生和價值觀，在空檔年中很可能可以發展出新的生活技能或找到隱藏的熱愛事物。

最後，給正在考慮空檔年的人一些建議，在事前大量做功課並且向嘗試過空檔年的人尋求建議。控制好預算並且花時間好好做計劃。保持心胸開闊，讓自己多方嘗試新事物。最後，記得享受每個當下！

Have you tried online dating?

With technology developing rapidly, ways of communication have greatly changed. Nowadays, online dating is more popular than ever. Tons of dating websites and apps have been invented to meet public's needs. All you need to do is fill in personal information to introduce yourself and upload a few photos.

Advantages of online dating? It's a way for you to acquaint with people outside your existing social network. And according to the information people fill in, you are likely to find people with similar background, values, interests and preferences within a short period of time.

Nevertheless, there are also drawbacks and limitations. For instance, the endless and unlimited swipes and selecting make individuals to commoditize potential partners. People may become picky. Unlimited supply of choice also means it's harder for people to make commitments. In addition, chatting with someone through the internet before meeting in real life can also cause individuals build up unrealistic expectations. Besides, people often lie on their profile.

Online dating sites or apps are, after all, just a platform. In the end, there's no right or wrong about it, just whether it's suitable for you or not.

你試過網路交友嗎？

隨著科技迅速發展，現代的通訊交流方式大大的改變了。現今，網路交友比以往更受歡迎，市面上出現了大量的交友網站和軟體以迎合大眾的需求，你需要做的，就只有填寫一些個人資訊和上傳幾張照片。

網路交友的優點？如果想認識平日社交圈以外的人，這會是一個好方法，而且，根據人們填寫的資訊，在網路上很可能可以快速的找到跟自己有相似背景、價值觀、興趣和嗜好的人。

然而，網路交友也存在著一些缺點和限制。舉例來說，無止盡也無限量的「左右滑」和選擇的過程可能讓人不知不覺中把潛在伴侶商品化，人們也可能會因此變得挑剔。無限量供應的選擇也意味著對於人們而言，許下承諾將會更加困難。另外，在現實生活中與某人見面前先在網路上聊天，可能會造成人們無意間在心中建立許多不切實際的期許。更不用說人們常常會在自己的檔案上撒謊了。

交友網站或軟體終究只是一個平台，到頭來，這個平台本身並不存在是非對錯，只是它適不適合你而已。

An education

Jenny is a unique, elegant young girl whose academic performances are well enough to possibly enter in Oxford. She stands out from her peers. The story begins as she encounters David, a charming sophisticated middle-age man.

She quickly falls in love with him. David expands Jenny's world. He takes her to fancy restaurants, talks about classical music and art with her, and even takes her to Paris for sightseeing. The delightful experiences Jenny share with David soon make her determine to drop out her studies and get married to him. Her values have greatly changed. However, later on, Jenny finds out that David is actually already married and he lies about his occupation and many other things. According to his wife, David used to have many affairs with other women as well. David disappears and abandons her in the end. A seemingly romantic story turns into a tragedy.

Jenny, heart-broken, returns to school, focuses on her studies and get into Oxford eventually. Her experience with David cures her urge for sophistication. By the time she is in university, she wants nothing more than to date decent, kind boys her own age.

名媛教育

珍妮是一個獨特而優雅的年輕女孩,她的學業成績優秀到足以讓她有機會進入牛津大學就讀。她在同儕中特別突出。故事從她邂逅一個充滿魅力而世故的中年男子大衛展開。

珍妮很快便愛上了大衛。他拓展了她的世界。他帶她上高級餐廳、和她談古典音樂和藝術,甚至帶她到巴黎觀光。和大衛相處的愉快經驗很快讓她下定決心拋棄學業並嫁給他,至此,她的價值觀已經和過去不同了。然而,不久後,珍妮發現大衛其實早就是有婦之夫,他同時也對自己的職業和很多事撒謊。根據大衛老婆的說法,他其實以前也和很多女人有過婚外情。大衛最後消失,拋下了珍妮。表面上看來的浪漫童話其實是一場悲劇。

心碎的珍妮重拾了學業,並努力讀書最後進入了牛津就讀。和大衛的這段過往治好了她曾經對世故的強烈渴望。當她進入大學後,珍妮只想和正直善良的同齡男生交往。

原來如此 系列 E228

玩遊戲學單字！英文中級單字
藏在格子裡：輕鬆戰勝英檢中級

國外最流行的猜謎遊戲，玩遊戲輕鬆學英檢中級單字！

作　　　者	捷徑文化語言企編小組◎著
顧　　　問	曾文旭
社　　　長	王毓芳
編輯統籌	耿文國、黃璽宇
主　　編	吳靜宜、姜怡安
執行編輯	吳佳芬
美術編輯	王桂芳、張嘉容
法律顧問	北辰著作權事務所　蕭雄淋律師、幸秋妙律師

初　　版	2020年07月
出　　版	捷徑文化出版事業有限公司
電　　話	（02）2752-5618
傳　　真	（02）2752-5619

定　　價	新台幣300元／港幣100元
產品內容	1書

總 經 銷	采舍國際有限公司
地　　址	235 新北市中和區中山路二段366巷10號3樓
電　　話	（02）8245-8786
傳　　真	（02）8245-8718

港澳地區總經銷	和平圖書有限公司
地　　址	香港柴灣嘉業街12號百樂門大廈17樓
電　　話	（852）2804-6687
傳　　真	（852）2804-6409

▶本書部分圖片由 Shutterstock、freepik 圖庫提供。

捷徑 Book站

現在就上臉書（FACEBOOK）「捷徑BOOK站」並按讚加入粉絲團，
就可享每月不定期新書資訊和粉絲專享小禮物喔！

http://www.facebook.com/royalroadbooks
讀者來函：royalroadbooks@gmail.com

國家圖書館出版品預行編目資料

玩遊戲學單字！英文中級單字藏在格子裡：
輕鬆戰勝英檢中級／捷徑文化語言企編小組著.
-- 初版. -- 臺北市：捷徑文化, 2020.07
　面；　公分（原來如此：E228）
ISBN 978-986-5507-29-9(平裝)

1. 英語　2. 詞彙

805.1892　　　　　　　　　　　109006442